The Ajnir

The Ajnir

M.P. GUNDERSON

TURNING
STONE
PRESS

First published in 2012 by
Turning Stone Press, an imprint of
Red Wheel/Weiser, LLC
With offices at:
665 Third Street, Suite 400
San Francisco, CA 94107
www.redwheelweiser.com

ISBN: 978-1-61852-034-0

Cover design by Jim Warner

Printed in the United States of America
10 9 8 7 6 5 4 3 2 1

Contents

Cast of Characters

Annod – Nadan's boss at the acron mine in Valyna
Cropaayaa – ajnir who studies uriel in Kira Mandi
Gahea – Toruna's maidservant in Simkada
Gooriom – the first ancient ajnir of Urshan Dai
Jagar – a miner in Valyna
Jali – Quilli man in Istandria
Kaitone – a demonic entity from the Mazag
Kaji – a Drogham nomad
Kalaso – librarian in the Wheel of Thought
Karam – Nadan's brother
Korbluun – ajnir whom Nadan meets in Kira Mandi
Laki – female magic child being who guides the Anatami
Luspen – planetary ruler of Terr'an
Manalk – Nadan's ajnir teacher
Mavblo – Simkada's army general
Nadan – central protagonist, an ajnir
Naria – Nadan's friend, whom he meets in Valyna
Pnav'Kle – Quilli woman who guides Nadan
Quizag – a Drogham nomad
Quizil – long-distance weaponry chief for the Simkadan army
Ranum – friend of Nadan's from Simkada
Sazm – Manalk's telepathic pet moth
Shakul – Anatami tribal member
Simrulde – female ajnir of Valyna

Speaker – a type of oracle contacted through contact with arthanti in the Dinjin

Surya – ajnir in Valyna, who runs the Quenna Corp., a powerful organization in the metropolis

Talili – the planet keeper of Urshan Dai

Ternaz – a Mandian miner in Valyna

Toruna – ajnir, friend of Manalk's in Simkada

Xaka – chief of ground warfare for the Simkadan army

Zalaam – the second planetary ruler of Urshan Dai, who escaped into the Dinjin

Chapter 1

The Kaitone

Like a sleeping animal, Simkada lay quiet. Wind had blown up from the east on this evening, sometimes tearing the pavilions and tents of nomads camped out on the Kiopic Desert outside the city. But the towering white walls that protected the city from ancient marauders retained the wind to a lull, despite the maelstrom outside its edges. On a quiet lane within the city, inside a kaaraadruun hut, a man named Manalk, an oracle from Kira Mandi, and a boy named Nadan sat across each other around a stone, knee high table. On the table in front of them, a small lumin-spire, a glass lighting device, had begun to run low on fuel, its fractured light ebbing into patterns of faint amber. The old man's eyes beamed sadly but calmly in the low light, as he pulled a glass box from a piece of linen cloth at his feet. The box contained a small silver moth, the size of a coin, with three red spots on its wing and a small green, faceted gem.

"Is that a pet?" asked the boy.

"An aid in what we are doing here. So you have consulted the oracles here?"

The boy fidgeted in his seat, still staring at the moth, flexing its wings within the glass box in quiet precision.

"Yes. They had nothing to say strangely. My family doesn't trust oracles from Kira Mandi such as yourself generally speaking. You said this oracle originates out of Time earlier. What do you mean by that?"

"In a sense, but rather I should say that it relates to another universe all together. That may be its advantage."

The man dipped his index finger into the glass box, stared at the moth as if he was having a conversation with it, then touched his marble white finger to the green gem in the container.

"Trees, trees" the man murmured to himself.

"Trees?" asked Nadan.

And, then the man appeared into go in a sort of trance. His eyebrows limped shut quietly for a minute, and for almost a minute his head rocked slowly, gently, from side to side in a very methodical rhythm, his bald head with a lightning bolt tattoo drowsing deeply into his chest. Nadan felt more nervous but also more awkward, and he wondered if this would answer the very dreadful question the man had come to his kaarraardruun hut to answer.

After almost a minute of this unusual behavior, the man re-opened his brownish black eyes widely, shuddered, and glanced around his room, as if he was bewildered where he was.

"The Speaker has unfortunate news for you," said Kira Mandi oracle, after he seemed to come to his senses. "Your brother is no longer alive. But in the

Ethereal Realm of Dinjin, the place where the oracles known as Speakers dwell, they don't really speak of the living and dead, as you might say. Rather, they would say transferred. I use the gem on my finger to speak with them. It's known as an arthanti."

"Dead?" said Nadan, coughing. For some reason, he took this statement more calmly than he would have expected.

"He's in the After-World, as they say here. He was running in a field, even as we speak, which should bring some comfort to you."

For a moment, Nadan lost his composure, but as if some force was compressing mind back into focus, he became calm again. He pondered this reading a while before answering.

"You are certain of this?" he asked finally.

"Yes. Isn't it true your brother had a cresecent scar on his shoulder? That would prove the accuracy of the reading, I'm sorry to say. There is more going on here, though the Speakers weren't able to tell me all."

"I see," said Nadan, with a tear running down his eyelid, as he glanced out the window at the bright light of afternoon, for he had seen his brother, Karam, get that scar when he was young from falling on a piece of shattered glass on the cobble stone streets of Simkada.

The old man placed the moth back in the bag at his feet, then stared at the ground despondently, before murmuring to himself something in Mandian, the language of Kira Mandi.

"How did he die?" asked Nadan, finally.

The old man drummed his hands on the table in front of them for a second.

"He was murdered," he said, after a long pause, "but by no entity of this world we live in."

～

Two days later, Karam's body lay out on a barrow outside the eastern city walls, where the tombs and ashes of millions of Simkadans now lay, some dating back thousands of years. For miles, the beige, earthen mounded graves stretched eastward into the dust-blown, time-beaten desert that bordered Simkada. Twirls of smoke and incense, tabaci and vanil, curled around his brother's form, sheltered by an open-sided ivory-colored pavilion. Nadan and his family offered prayers and burnt offerings of kuireme leaves to Urum, the great solar deity most venerated in Simkada. They sang and reflected on Karam's life. But Nadan felt no relief and privately he sensed the disturbance of his close relatives. Both of his parents had died in an anti-gravity vehicle accident when he was only four years of age. And now Karam had passed under equally peculiar circumstances (few deaths resulted from the silently levitating vehicles). This was more tragedy than had been visited on any other family around, and everyone knew it, but no one mentioned this fact at the funerary rites because it was considered impolite in Simkadan society to even mention such a calamity to a family.

As for the cause of Karam's death, it was still not clear, but the coroners had reported a small hole in his heart, which was probably the reason. It was a strange, rare health disorder which would have caused such a problem, but even stranger was how the boy's body was discovered. Nadan's uncle Gizal had found the body with no note on a steel litter outside his kaaraadruun hut the morning before. Gizal was suspicious that Karam had been accidentally or intentionally killed, and that the killers, whoever they were, became guilty over what they had done and decided to leave the body with his family. Gizal, who had been through the war with the northern city of Valyna and had seen many deaths, had called the Port Authority immediately about his suspicions. The Port Authority, however, pointed to the coroner's report, which claimed the death was of natural causes, and decided not to pursue the incident as a murder.

At the funeral rites, as he spoke, Gizal broke the usually formal and reserved funeral tradition in Simkada and noted that he did not believe that the death was natural.

"While we can only conjecture about what happened, I knew Karam's health was known for being impeccable," the brusque, sometimes tactless man mentioned as he was speaking, losing some of his typical composure. But he stopped there, even as his wife next to him made a sudden hiss of disapproval.

For most of the funeral rites, Nadan stayed quiet, feeling lifeless inside and staring at the ground with his brown hood tucked way down over his face, not wanting to look at his brother's pale, wan face.

∽

The realms beneath have struck a terrible chord. The links are meeting once again, but both the worlds on each side of us are threading what they are, or want to be, into us, and making us what they are. The lower wants the higher to be pulled down. The higher wants to be higher than itself. In this way, we live in a partial portion.

Nadan heard these words running through his mind later that night, when the birds of Simkada lay quiet and he was writing his thoughts out about the whole ordeal. He felt as if he was being partially pulled into a dream state. He set his pen down and walked to the window, staring at the flame-red graffiti on the wall next door which said: "Bravery is nothing until you show it."

The subtle voice continued: *The gates and also the keys are invisible. Everything is a gateway and not an end itself. Time is slowing at the lower, and running quicker and more silently at the upper. I heard a river in each and every context, and it went and stopped, the thoughts of all beings in all their contexts.*

Nadan returned to his seat, a bed of cushions, and ran his hands along his shaven scalp, and then, he heard the whispering voice say, as if more directly to him: *You can hear me?* Nadan felt alarmed at this point, and his hand trembled a bit.

I am listening. You heard my conversation. You can reply.

Nadan felt he didn't know how to reply. Still, he remained a bit quiet, thinking what to say when he did make a reply.

Project your thought, the voice said.

Project my thought?

The voice seemed to laugh, in this low golden whisper.

You see. You did it.

～

The next night, around the same time, the voice returned. But this time it was clearer and more palpable.

The grief is difficult but you are letting it go well.
There is not necessarily any virtue in grieving too much.

Nadan waited hesitantly, listening to the quiet air of the night, near the door leading into the garden behind his hut.

Who is this? he asked.

Who do you think?

Manalk.

Not too hard, is it?

Nadan almost gave himself a sly grin, and for a moment, he felt a great relief flood through his being. He listened for almost a minute and after that time, he got the picture in his mind of the man, sitting at a table, a stone table somewhere, but the picture was vague and not crisp. It took him almost a minute to assimilate what was happening, but when he did, he said:

I had no idea you could speak this way.

Manalk's mind seemed to quiver for a second, but already Nadan was getting a grasp of his own psychic sensibility. Manalk's mind was like philosophical clouds, floating in his mind, cool and steady, distantly proximate.

It was as I feared: your brother was killed by a Kaitone, a ghastly creature from the Mazag, a dark universe that suspends like a balloon around this world, like Dinjin, telepathed Manalk, after a moment, during which he seemed busy with something else happening in his room. *They were afraid of your brother or your family, or so it seems, the Kaitone. The Port Authority of Simkada is worried: not in 400 years have they seen a Kaitone killing here, though they don't understand it.*

What do you mean? For a second, Nadan thought he could see Manalk's white, round, moon-like face, bereft and taciturn, and nearby, three silver moths, playing near his ear nearby.

Four hundred years ago, there was a wave of some 48 killings in Simkada. Not unusual for those grim times perhaps, the oracle returned, *but the strange thing about these murders was that there were no signs of bodily injury in the victims' bodies. The Kaitone use a special form of spellcraft, known as a meta, to transmute flesh and matter to inflict bodily harm. This is exactly what happened to your brother. The Port Authority was in possession of your brother's form for a while investigating it. They still know nothing of the Mazag or the Kaitone.*

Nadan's eyes strayed to the window, where the sound of gorlon bird cries echoed along the cobble stones. He had, of course, heard already from Manalk that his brother was killed by some sort of inter-dimensional, though the oracle didn't specify a name. The horrific idea was so troubling and disturbing to him that he had found himself diverting his thoughts constantly: to regular events and actions that had nothing to do with the situation. He said nothing in reply. Instead, he thought of his brother and his family for a while, and how he had felt the entire time during this whole ordeal a sense of estrangement from them – almost like he was not in their world of customs and obligatory acts. A growing sensation that he felt out of place within his culture had been enveloping him ever since last spring, and this recent tragedy almost intensified these emotions.

You are none of those things, telepathed Manalk. *But it's actually a good sign. You just don't remember who you are.*

A good sign? Nadan replied, feeling a bit embarrassed.

Many of us ajnir have the same problem. We feel akin to society but not part of what it thinks. We are part of a river but not its contexts.

That sounds like that voice I was hearing last night in my mind.

It was some poetry I was reading from the Dinjin.

Nadan went to the door of his hut, opened it, and stared outside for a moment into the garden. There were a few children playing with some dice in the street beyond, but he couldn't see the old man anywhere. Outside, he could hear the bells marking the time of midnight clanging in the humid air of the summer night. The trees along the sides of the street were sighing in the night wind. Above them, the ancient vehicular tunnels that twisted and turned through the city were lighted with a crimson glow. The tunnels were built in ancient times to deal with the city's overpopulation problem. Tourists sometimes traveled across the Kiopic Desert to the north of Simkada to visit the tunnels, but locals inside the city thought they were an eyesore and walked past them with little interest. Nadan stared at the white and red lium and goli flowers that hemmed in each side of the walkway that led into the cobblestone street.

Those flowers smell nice, telepathed Manalk.

You can smell them? replied Nadan.

I can also see them quite clearly. This is actually the first time I've seen a goli flower. They don't grow in the Valyna or Kira Mandi.

Nadan bent down and picked one of the red flowers and smelled it. Some of the petals fell off the bulbous, large flower and scattered in the wind at his feet.

Kurieme trees grow in Valyna, but there aren't many. They are more plentiful in Simkada. I just wish there were more trees on our planet.

There's not enough water, answered Nadan, glumly.

Thousands of years ago, the Kiopic Desert was not a desert but a huge forest. Water was much more plentiful on Urshan Dai.

What is an ajnir? The named stirred Nadan's mind for some reason. Had he heard it somewhere before? It sounded mystical and far away, exotic.

You like the word? It's from Mandian, one of its oldest languages, the Ganir dialect. Secret is the first syllable. Nir means worker. As I was explaining to you before, there are three universes, the Mazag and Dinjin and this world, which interpolate. It has something to do with that, but I can't say more.

You can't say more?

As I said, the Kaitone use metas. Some of them restrict me from what I'm trying to tell you. All I can tell you is that you are no longer in danger because I have made them forget about you for the time being with my own metas.

Chapter 2

The Arthanti

Nadan crept to the edge of the curtain of his house and stared outside. Over the desert to the east, the Light-Star was beginning its sleep, descending into colors of oceanic purple and red sand as it set. The street, with the brown clay wall across the street stained with graffiti, was painted red with its color.

Still, no one was there, though he had been having this feeling someone was watching him all the time, an unfriendly man in a brown robe. He had seen the man twice now in his dreams—standing there just below the window near the graffiti with a scimitar in his anemic hand.

Nadan went back over to his seat and read a phrase from a book of poetry, an ancient Mandian poet he was reading named Sarir.

> From the moment, a glare, a tortured illness.
> Illuminated is the stillness; it becomes the resilience,
> At least some resilience.

43 ghals. He read his timepiece, suddenly remembering that he had forgotten he was going to meet Manalk later that night at 44. He quietly shut

down the lumin-globes that were keeping the temperature a little bit higher than he preferred in his kaaraadruun hut. The temperature dropped immediately, as the ducts in his wall, which had devices that determined his favored temperature, siphoned the air out of the chamber.

That is significant, said a voice like a silver reed in his mind.

Whether it was Manalk, he wasn't certain. But he felt like it was not, and when he asked the voice for further explanation, he only heard a muffled response. But he had to go soon, and, after a minute of listening to the stillness of the evening air, he decided to leave, knowing Manalk was up at his cave at the base of the Thuresce Mountains as usual. Three turns of the double moons had passed since he had met Manalk, and the man had virtually shunned the civilization of the city, living in a remote cavern near the outlying roads of Simkada, at the base of Zxe Mountain, the closest peak to the city. There was one sole Kurieme tree in that area, just at the entrance of the cave tree with two large V-shaped branches protruding up from its main stem. Save for a few hikers and skiffs, the path leading up to the mountain was isolated and almost never visited.

Taking only a canteen on one shoulder, Nadan sidled out on the street in front of his hut. The evening was now darkening, and the city's lumin-globes, red and yellow and brightly lit, had already been turned on to light the way for walkers. Kurieme trees were spaced every few hundred yards along the cobblestone road. Above him, the great tunnels over the city were gray and dimly reflecting the light of lumin-globes below.

As Nadan shuffled along the road towards the city's gates westward, a thin woman appeared around the corner of one of the streets. Black hair traced all the way to her lower back. Her eyes were moist and black, and she had the deep scent of tunivial. She immediately pulled up alongside him and eyed him probingly.

"A little late for trolling the desert," she said. "Is that where you are headed? I can see you have travelling in your eyes."

"Not too far," he said, not wanting to explain where he was going.

"The Drogham can be dangerous these days," she said, referring to the nomads that wandered and camped to the north of Simkaca. "I hear they murdered a man last week, but I see you aren't afraid."

"I hadn't heard that. But I don't plan to go that far north. I'm meeting somebody near the western gates."

"A girl?"

"No, a friend."

She swung her black hair to one side and pulled in closer to his chest, stopping him as they walked.

"You can come stay with me tonight, if you want."

"You charge, don't you?"

"Forty-five."

Nadan had never been with a prostitute before, and though he had never liked the idea, he felt suddenly more drawn and attracted to the girl than when he had first met her. At that moment, a yellow moth fluttered in his ear and seemed to whisper something telepathically in his ear: *This is not what it seems.*

The girl suddenly became scared. Her eyes rolled and she pulled away from him, putting her left fingertip to her mouth, as if she was thinking deeply. She seemed deeply troubled; then she turned to him and said, "Do you want to come with or no?" She was less comfortable though than before, more upset.

"I'm meeting a friend," he said, staring at her strangely. "What is wrong?"

The girl look at him timidly, then hurried down the side street, past the glare of the overarching yellow lumin-globe on the corner, where a sign for an inn hung wearily over the road that read: "Caloba."

That was right, said the moth.

I didn't know moths were psychic, he replied.

Some are, some aren't. It was now hovering up near the base of the Caloba sign. *I was giving you a message from Manalk, but I see you needed no direction. That girl was trying to kill you. She had several metas on you, trying to pull you into a room, so we were a bit worried for you.*

Don't tell me. Manalk said I was safe. And why isn't he telling me himself?

Over the mountain range, the white radiance of the moon Kindri was bathing the landscape. The moth paused in the light before answering, fluttered between him and the moon, before saying:

Moogies, another Mazag being. They intervene between you and the sender, either blocking the telepaths conversing or conveying totally opposite messages to what the person intended. There's a whole bunch of them between you and Manalk right now. They are on the side of the Kaitone.

Almost .3 ghals later, just after 44, Nadan entered the cave of Manalk. He had been to the place only twice in the last three months (Manalk usually came to his hut inside the city), and Manalk had set the place up better. Two rows of lavender cushions lined each side of the cave. The walls bore two colored tapestries, with intertwining symbols, gilded figure eights with radiating silver concentric circles emanating out from the central symbol. This, Manalk had told him, was the major insignia of the ajnir, which was also used by the Wheel of Thought, the central authority of the ajnir based in Valyna.

In the center of the cave was a tall light, a transparent lumin-spire climbing four feet or so in the humid air. Manalk wasn't there, and by the light of the wick at the base of the lumin-spire, he thought he had probably been gone a few hours, since those particular wicks couldn't be shut off once they were lit. Nadan walked to the back of the cave and was about to sit in one of the cushions on the far right of the wall when he noticed the stone table at the back of the cave. On it was a silver container he had seen Manalk carrying when they had first met.

The arthanti! he thought, and even as he thought about it, he wanted to use it. He walked over to the container, near to the cage where the ajnir kept his gorlon birds, and opened it, his hands trembling a little with excitement, for he had never tried an oracle like this before. Inside, he could see that it was not the same crystal he had seen before; this one was crimson, not the green arthanti he had seen Manalk use during the oracle reading. He reached out and touched it for a second, and even as he did, he saw in his mind a circular ring of high trees and grass and what looked like a man with a white braided beard on his chest under a tomb of glass in the center of the ring of trees.

"It's beautiful," he whispered, out loud, but even as he did, he fell over unconscious.

∼

"It's lucky you are still alive," said Manalk, when Nadan came to.

The Light-Star was peering in through the entrance of the cave. The lumin-spire was burning low to a light amber color, hardly going, except as a coolant, since it could also be used to regulate temperature. Manalk was feeling his pulse, and examining the lines of his palm very carefully. But his eyes weren't worried.

"Most of the oracles around here would yell at you for doing such a thing," he said, after a minute, standing up. "I think you know better than to tamper with exotic oracular devices, since they can be dangerous for the untrained. But that just shows it wasn't entirely your fault."

"It was the Kaitone, wasn't it?" Nadan said, having a sudden intuitional impulse.

"True. They put that thought in your head just before you got here to touch the peering gem. It was stronger than the green one, too strong for you in fact at your level of things. The same goes with that girl you met on the road. I'm seeing now it was you they were after all along. Your brother wasn't such a threat, but they were trying to deeply upset you for some reason. What that reason is I'm still uncertain. The Kaitone are good at hiding their tracks, too good, in fact."

Manalk leaned down and felt his pulse again, then stood up, stroking his chin and feeling his bare white arm with his fingers. Nadan watched him intently, and he felt somehow the experience of touching the gem made him extraordinarily present. The red and brown streaked walls seemed to have this haloed glow about them, and the light of lumin-spire crystal seemed somehow deeper and more interesting.

"That is good, though," said Manalk, looking at him intently in the eyes, as he did when he was scanning his mind and his dreams from the night before for information. "The arthanti felt you, and you felt it. That at least is a good sign, though you were untried in what you were doing. There's a being linked into the arthanti from the Dinjin, living, breathing, pulsing, just as you are. Her name is Na. For a time, she lets you see what she sees, the woods and planets she walks through. For a while, when you touch the crystal, your minds merge, and she feels you and your world. Sometimes, the user upsets Na, and she leaves them shaken and feeling terrible inside about all the bad things they've done. You weren't precise about what you were pursuing there, but the experience wasn't too bad, though it was much too strong for you and might have collapsed your lungs, if I had not intervened."

"It was a strange place I saw, but beautiful. I saw trees and a white stone tomb, it looked like," said Nadan.

"A second or so, I noticed," said Manalk. "Not too much, but the vibration was too strong."

"It was a strange place for a tomb, and clear glass. Do the Dinjin all bury their dead that way? And who was that man?"

"The Ancient Sleeper," said Manalk, pursing his lips. "He sleeps in that tomb, but it's not really a tomb. It's more of a sleeping chamber. He's from the Old World. His name is Abeorn."

"So he's from Urshan Dai? How can that be? I didn't think anyone here could live in the Dinjin.

"The ajnir today can't do that," said Manalk. "In the Old World, some were able to slip between the dimensions from time to time and stay permanently in the Dinjin. The dimensional veils were more open back then, and the more advanced ajnir could move between the Dinjin and our world with freedom."

"What caused the veils to thicken?"

"The Wheel of Thought doesn't know. All we know is that the windows between the Dinjin and our planet open and close, like flowers, in cycles over thousands of years. Abeorn was able to slip into the Dinjin for a long while in the Old World. After being there for a few months, he fell in love with a woman on Haalathrom, the planet you just saw for a moment. Nafiri, the planet keeper or type of deity of Haalathrom, didn't like it that Abeorn wanted to stay permanently in the Dinjin and be with her. She kept telling him it was not his world, and that he should return to Urshan Dai. He refused her advice, and she was not able to force him to return, so she cast a sleeping enchantment spell on him. He has been sleeping in that world for thousands of years, dreaming, barely alive, but never waking. The planet keepers guard over their planets and take care of their inhabitants. Nafiri didn't want any racial intermixing between the people of Urshan Dai and the inhabitants of Haalathrom, since it caused a half-breed of Urshan Dai people that was too aggressive and also too powerful at metas. This is how the Kaitones came about."

"There are lights in this cave," said Nadan, glancing up at the ceiling of the cave. "What are they?" Above him, green, red, and yellow lights were flashing across his vision, quiet lasers almost in the dark light but more subtle and refined to his vision. But above that, in the far corner of the cave where the gorlon birds were clacking their beaks, there appeared to be a tiny orb of black energy.

"Those are anamatis," said Manalk. "They are thought particles, the thoughts of all living beings. Those anamatis around us are your thoughts and my thoughts. Your experience with the Dinjin has allowed you to see them. But that black energy there is a problem, a moogie, I think, listening in on us."

When Nadan glanced back at the corner, the black orb was gone.

Chapter 3

The Departure of Manalk

Two days later, a nightmarish storm was brooding over the Kiopic Desert, to the east of the city. Lightning gouged the air over the desert every few seconds. Thunder rolled and echoed off the Thuresce Mountains to the east, and the Drogham nomads, who camped out on the desert outside the city, were huddled under their tents for cover.

"A dragon and an antelope," said Ranum, rolling the silver and black dice on the floor of Nadan's kaaraadruun hut.

"You win," said Nadan.

"The antelope always beats the snake," Ranum said, tossing his gold-colored hair to one side.

Nadan smiled and picked up the dice in his hand, rolling them over and over skillfully in his sweaty palm. They had been playing ralka for hours, but while he always enjoyed the game, he felt strangely uneasy. The shutters of his windows were rattling against the mud walls of his hut. The gorlon birds, perched on the roofs of the huts that lined his street, were hooting in fear at the impending storm. It didn't rain much in Simkada, but when it did, it was a major event in the city. Residents of the city placed large metal basins outside their huts to help catch the water. Children played in the rain for hours, and the city officials shut down all work so that people could collect water.

"We should go out and watch the storm under the lee of your hut," said Ranum, after taking a sip of ghal at his feet. The herbal beverage was a relaxant. Simkadans loved drinking it together socially, and Ranum was virtually addicted to the drink.

Together, they moved outside into the garden behind Nadan's hut and sat under the massive slanting blackened roof, which jutted down at an angle from the main mud structure of the building. Two Kurieme trees in the middle of the small garden were swaying anxiously in the wind stirring through the city.

"A thunderstorm," said Nadan, sniffing the air. "Very rare."

"I hope it doesn't kill any trees," said Ranum. "The city officials are often worried about this sort of storm."

Nadan sat in the wooden chair, still and silent for a moment, pondering the black cumulus cloud billowing on the northern horizon.

I feel something is wrong, he telepathed to his friend after a moment.

Storms like this can give you that feeling. Ranum's telepathy was getting clearer and stronger every day. His friend had awoken to his identity as an ajnir soon after he had. Ranum was sitting on the other chair in the back patio, scratching his scalp with his left hand.

Over their heads a flock of black-winged navkles flew in a V-formation. They were flying westward, completely silent overhead, away from the storm. All Nadan could hear was the rustle of the birds' wings overhead.

"Navkles," said Ranum out loud. "Dratted things. I wish they wouldn't come back."

"They take cover in Tyune Hills during storms," said Nadan. He glanced at the storm cloud, brooding dark on the horizon, and then he felt Manalk's telepathing in his mind, weakened, almost anemic.

Valyna . . .

The old man's mind seemed interrupted by some sort of static. Then, Nadan felt a deep sense of depression wash over him.

You are in trouble? asked Nadan, but the only response he felt was the wind sighing through the trees in the garden.

Next to him, Ranum blanched in his chair.

Nadan, I just saw him. Soldiers, Valynan soldiers, are standing around him. He's tied to a table.

Ranum's far viewing using his telepathy was much better than Nadan's. He could watch events unfolding from a distance, like on an electronic screen. Nadan could see only faint flashes of his master's angst-filled face, still and placid as usual but barely suppressing some sort of deep agony or inner struggle. Together, they ran out through the center of Nadan's hut and out to the street. Outside, merchants selling trinkets, necklaces, and gems had set up long wooden tables. They were hastily moving the objects into wooden boxes.

"Where is he?" asked Nadan, stopping near one of the purple-clothed tables.

Ranum paused for a moment and pressed his fingers against his head. The wind was blowing up the cloth on the tables, and metallic objects on them were rattling and clinking.

"Hard to say. It's dark wherever he is."

"We'll try the cave," said Nadan.

They moved quickly through the crowded streets, unable to run in the mob of people shuffling past in huge throngs. The rain was now falling more heavily, and Ranum and Nadan were both starting to get wet. Lightning lashed at the horizon, and thunder rolled off the Thuresce Mountains. They were soon outside of the towering white gates of the city and running on the slippery mud path up the foot of Zxe Mountain. Rainwater was running in tiny, murky streams down the path, and often they had to run on the elevated sides of the path to avoid the fast-moving, ankle-deep water which was coursing down the path. It was now pouring, and the rain blinded them as they ran.

In a few minutes, they reached the mouth of the cave where Manalk lived. It was a small, craggy opening in the side of a cliff at the base of the mountain. The soil was sandy at the front of the cave, which allowed no vegetation to grow around the entrance, but there were small shrubs on either side of the cave's mouth. Even as they approached, they felt a heavy energy hanging about it, repelling them away.

"I don't feel like going in," said Ranum, stopping in his tracks.

"Me neither," said Nadan, strangely.

Together, they turned around and began clambering down the rock piles that led to the cave, carefully avoiding the muddy currents of water running down the slope. As they did, Nadan felt a prick, like a needle, in his back. He sat down on the stone in front of him, a red slab of felmir angling down the mountain slope. He felt sleepy suddenly, and he felt his limbs becoming paralyzed. In a few seconds, he lost consciousness.

∿

When he came to, Nadan was in a cage. It was a cage he had seen many times before: it was the same one Manalk had used to house his pet gorlon birds. The cage was in the back of Manalk's cave, but the birds were gone. Outside in the cave, around the corner of the nook he was in, he could hear the sounds of men digging with shovels. As he watched the shadows of the men flitting along the cave's walls, a lumin-globe sputtered out, immersing the entire place for a few seconds into pitch-blackness.

When the globe flickered on again, a wiry-looking soldier appeared around the corner of the hollow and gently opened the metal door of the cage, extending a small green lamp toward Nadan's face. In the light of it, Nadan could see a wearied halcyon countenance, surveying him with birdlike, penetrating, precise eyes. What perplexed Nadan was that he discerned no thoughts in the man's mind with his telepathy, a fact which led him to suspect the man was also ajnir, like himself, and thus able to ward off the psychic invasions in some way.

"Do you feel a tingling sensation along your skin?" The man's gravelly voice sounded like razors cutting the stagnant air.

Nadan nodded his head. He could feel a gleam of thought within the man's mind. It felt like worry or fear, but he still could ascertain no details about it. His first thought was this attack on him was the result of the Kaitone, similar to the prostitute in the city, but this time, there was no verification of what was happening. The moth of Manalk, Sazm, did not return this time to lend him help.

After a few more moments of scanning his eyes, the man's muscular shape disappeared into the alternating, chaotic rhythms of flashing lights. Nadan's sight was still blurry from the sleeping drug they had given him; the air wiggled in waves around the cage, but all around him, he could see gorlon bird feathers, red and purple and white, swirling in the air, as a wind from outside gusted into the cave.

Outside the cage, the sounds of digging and pickaxes had stopped. Nadan could hear the soldiers talking in muted whispers to each other, shuffling through papers, and tinkering with cans and metal tins and pots outside. How long had he lost consciousness? He had no way of knowing for sure.

After a few minutes, the soldier who had injected him with the drug threw open the cage door, its rusted hinges squeaking faintly against the sound of metal on stone in the background. In the darkness, Nadan, for some reason, was now able to get a quick glimpse of the man's brain and what was in it, as if the barrier that had blocked his psychic ability had suddenly dropped away. It was only a flash, and it didn't last for more than a few seconds, the image he saw. Embedded in the man's now-unveiled memory he saw Saaruun, his master, outside under the stars, on a mountainside somewhere in the desert.

The vision, the image harvested from the man's memory, faded slowly in Nadan's mind's eye. Nadan noticed the man with the pale face was standing over him again, his long black braided goatee outlined like the branches of a tree in the background light of the lumin-globe lamp outside in the cave. This time, someone else was at his side, a larger man, it looked like.

"Dafna, make him sleep some more," said the man, in a quiet, disturbed voice, tinged with emotion. "I don't want him to see any more of this."

Nadan felt the prick of a needle on his arm, as the larger man bent over him, wrapping large, rough fingers around his tricep. A few seconds later, his vision went dark again.

Chapter 4

The Voice of the Uriel

Outside Manalk's cave, the Kurieme trees were wet and glistening. The storm from the night before had passed, and it was now two hours past morning. The Light Star was glimmering red on the southern horizon, sending fractured rays through the indolent black storm clouds, which were now edging slowly eastward. On the desert on the outskirts of the city, Drogham nomads were taking down their rain pavilions and gathering up their water collection basins at the base of their tents.

"Look there," said Quizag, the Drogham, to his friend, Kaji, at his side. They were both standing at the mouth of Quizag's crimson tent.

Kaji stared toward Zxe Mountain, holding his hands up on one side of his face to shield his eyes from the blinding rays of the Light Star. At first, he could see nothing on the snow-peaked mountain, which cut the sky like a jagged knife.

"Do you mean those gorlon?" he asked. He was feeling impatient. He was busy with collecting water and didn't want to be bothered.

"No, lower," said Quizag.

Kaji scanned his eyes downward to the foothills of Zxe Mountain. There he saw a line of crimson dots, moving slowly along the tree-barren landscape.

"Use your far-seeing eye," said Quizag.

Kaji reached into the pockets along his pant leg and pulled out the device. With a quick movement, he pulled it up to his eye and stared into it. It took him a few moments to lock in on the line of red dots.

"What is it?" asked Quizag.

Kaji handed him the far-seeing eye. Quizag wasn't familiar with the device, and it took him almost a minute to figure out how to locate the dots on the horizon. Kaji helped him focus the lens. When it was ready, he saw a line of three red-uniformed men, running swiftly along the mountain. Even as he looked, he saw one trip and fall on the mountain path, then get up quickly and keep running.

"Valynan soldiers," he cried, angrily.

"It's an outrage," said Kaji.

"They know about the amnesty," said Quizag. "They know Simkadans will not stand for this."

Ten years ago, the war between Valyna and Simkada had ended. It was a fragile treaty, and trade between the two cities remained scarce. The major import from Valyna to Simkada was acron, the fuel which powered the city's anti-gravity skiffs, but beyond that, there was little interaction between the two cities, and the people of Valyna and Simkada shared a mutual dislike. Valynans often scoffed at Simkadans as outdated parvenus of the Old World Order. Simkadans were distrustful of the Valynan progressivism and the Valynans' restless pursuit of new technology and luxury.

The Drogham bartered with both cultures, but Quizag and Kaji and their families, though nomadic, tended to stay around Simkada more often than Valyna. While the Drogham remained culturally separate from the two cities' societies, camping out on the desert, all Drogham clans feared a breach of the amnesty between the two cities more than anything else, since it would upset their nomad existence and the bartering system between the Drogham and both cities.

"This will bring war," said Kaji, anxiously. "Valynan soldiers this deep into Simkadan territory."

He shook his head, as he took the far-seeing eye back from Quizag.

"Only if the city officials find out," said Quizag, folding the device and placing it back in his pant leg. "We shouldn't say anything about this. Simkadans would never stand for this."

Both Drogham men watched the line of red soldiers disappear around the edge of a pale white cliff in the foothills of Zxe Mountain, then they turned into Quizag's tent. Inside, they had collected several metal basins of water, and they splashed their faces in them before sitting down and staring into the fire pit in the middle of the living space.

But there were other eyes watching the Valynan soldiers, even as the two nomads went about their business. Inside Simkada's governing towers, watchmen saw the soldiers as they emerged from the cliffs and kept running. Immediately, they went down and told the city's military warden, who called a meeting of the city's top army officials.

"This is an express violation of Amnesty 343," said Mavblo, Simkada's chief army general.

He was a short man, with deep-set bristling azure eyes and a black mustache curling across his pale, almost anemic skin. On his chest, he wore the symbol of Simkada's army, a large golden serpent medallion twisted in three loops. The serpent was biting its tail. Two other men were sitting at a smoothly polished felmir table with him at the top of the city's governing tower: Quizil, the long-distance weaponry chief, and Xaka, chief of ground warfare.

"We should be coy," said Quizil. He was sitting at an angle to the table, one elbow resting on the stone table; his skinny, ashen fingers were propping up his chin. He had a cool, saturnine expression on his face.

"What do you mean?" asked Mavblo.

"We should send in some spies on Valyna first," said the young man. "We should find out what they were doing."

Mavblo tapped the gold ring on his right hand twice on the felmir table. His face was reflective and withdrawn. Quizil, who knew him well, noticed that he was much more introspective and pensive than usual.

"They were in the foothills of Zxe Mountain," said Mavblo, after a long pause. "They were looking for something there. Acron, perhaps. I wonder. We should scour around there first, then send in some spies to Valyna."

"We've seen Valynan soldiers a few times on the Quantan Way in the last few moon turns," said Xaka. "That's what our Drogham spies have told us. We should strike hard and fast and maybe reclaim

Simkada's northern territories. If we don't, Valyna will stretch its reach out farther."

"That would start open war," said Mavblo, grimly. "Valyna will not cede those lands easily."

"They are stronger," said Xaka. "Their weaponry is more advanced, but we have the shields."

In the last few years, Simkadan scientists had pioneered a new energy device which could physically repel men and vehicles from an entire area of the Simkadan army's choosing. Anyone entering the field of energy would feel himself pushed away by a subtle, yet powerful force. Using a remote control machine, Simkadan army leaders could set boundaries around an area using the shields and repel anyone they wanted from entering the field. The Simkadan army hadn't made the shields public yet, and Valyna leaders still knew nothing about the pioneering defense weaponry.

"I fear greater retaliation," said Mavblo, glancing out through the room's tiny oval window with a jaded expression. "The shield devices are few, and we certainly can't protect the entire city with them, as well as our entire borders. Valynan bombs are too powerful."

"It's true, but our forces are strong," said Xaka. "The city folk could live in the caves in the mountains during any bomb attacks, and the casualties could be few. If we use the shields we have strategically, we could own Valyna's territories within a few years."

~

Inside Manalk's cave, immersed in almost pure darkness, Nadan felt something like a hand, an invisible hand, brush against his shoulder. After it, he heard a voice, a very soft but firm voice in his mind, a voice which he couldn't understand. He looked around but saw nothing and no one around him. Outside, through the jagged mouth of the cave, he could see the sky glimmering like a sheet of scintillating amber energy, as the Light Star began its slow ascent over the horizon. Kindri was rising in the early stages of dawn, red streaked and crescent shaped.

He fumbled in the darkness for his canteen, and after finding it, sipped it slowly, letting his mind settle. A lumin-globe, a mind-sensored device that went on when a person woke, flickered on, bathing the cavern in a green ambiance. Even as it did, a sensation, almost like breath on his skin, flickered across his arm, and waves of light trembled in the air around him. The air was still again for a moment. Then, the air flickered again, and he saw what it was: a semi-transparent luminous being flickering along the intricately patterned red and green tapestries lining the cave's wall. He felt afraid for a moment, but then the emotion passed, as he realized intuitively how peacefully, how energetically the form of the apparition in front of him was interacting with his awareness.

The being reached out its pale, almost wan light beam of a hand and pressed it gently, delicately against his white-skinned face. Nadan felt a radiance, like a breath of peace, percolating into his consciousness, ameliorating his grief and despair, the origin of which he had forgotten.

The being pulled its hand back slowly and leaned forward, its transparent neck extending outward from its indistinct form, as it placed its forehead against his own with gentle reassurance. Nadan saw a world, a type of dazzling electric galaxy that was unimaginable in its brightness and clarity, penetrating into his forehead from inside the creature's facial area. For a moment, he wondered what this world was that he was seeing. He imagined that it was most likely the world that this being came from.

The being pulled itself upright again and said telepathically:

The inner light is bending . . . The words became broken . . . *is seeing us.*

Nadan thought it sounded as if it was speaking to some other entity, whom he could not himself see.

What do you want from me? he asked, telepathically.

The being moved its head closer, its face wiggling and shimmering like an otherworldly firework display.

It is not . . . design . . . the words became broken again.

The creature seemed to be coughing, or exhaling. And then it said, more deeply than before, so that its psychic voice trembled with power inside Nadan's mind: *Kira Mandi.*

Kira Mandi? Nadan replied back to it. *You want me to go to Kira Mandi?*

The creature seemed to nod its head in affirmation. A light wind, a breeze, flickered in through the air, but then he noticed it was not a breeze but a subtle wind of some sort, wafting in through the chamber. The being seemed to drift along this breeze of radiation, floating up to the ceiling, where it made a vague sort of graceful movement before vanishing into the stone ceiling.

Nadan lay back on his mat, wondering, thinking, and watching a pale mist shifting across Kindri's red streaks. He had never seen a uriel before, but he had read about them: strange apparitions, gibbering nonsensical riddles in the night. There was a subculture of thinkers across the planet who were convinced that the messages had some deep significance, but no one, as of yet, had come up with a unified theory of what the apparitions were or what their ultimate intent was. A feeling enveloped him suddenly that the uriel and the ajnir were somehow connected, yet he didn't know why he had such an intuition.

As he lay there, looking into the stars outside the mouth of the cave, he reflected on how he had gotten to Manalk's cave in the first place. He remembered being at Ranum's place for a while, and then leaving. But beyond that, he could recollect nothing of what happened the prior evening. And where were Ranum and Manalk now? Manalk almost never slept anywhere else than in his cave.

"There is a constant river of thoughts flowing between the veiling divides between universes," Manalk had explained. "Thoughts are carried by anamatis, and these inter-dimensional particles shuttle thoughts between the three multi-verses in a constant interchange of energies. Sometimes, the flow of Mazag increases in our world, and we experience wars, violence, and famines. At other times in history, the Dinjin flows stronger, and we see peace and prosperity reign on Urshan Dai."

These words of Manalk were echoing in Nadan's mind as he ambled down the foothills of Zxe Mountain later that night. He was using a historical meta on himself—which allowed him to review his past memories and conversations in vivid detail—to review his old master's teachings. The word *Mazag* had kept floating in his mind all night for some reason, and he had forgotten most of what Manalk had told him about that bleak and terrible universe. Inhabitants there were said to live on molten ash, and the planets in that dimension had little vegetation, if any, Manalk had said. He tried a mood-uplifting meta on himself, but it didn't work. The cold, despondent feeling that had been creeping on him all night continued to haunt his mind, as if it were some inevitable force in his mind or as if there were some imminent catastrophe of which he was somewhat prescient.

When he returned to his kaaraadruun hut, he played some music on his khorgatan guitar to distract his mind from the feeling. He organized a row of plants on the glass tables that stood near his window, overlooking a cobblestone alleyway beneath the windows of his small kaaraadruun-mud bedroom.

In the midst of these dark, heavy emotions, a dim but lucid realization began to dawn on him: Manalk was missing and not returning anytime soon.

Manalk often taught with actions, rarely with words. He sensed some sort of lesson here, but he wasn't sure.

Finally, he lay on the rug of his room and fell into a dozing sleep, in which he seemed partly aware of the room around him still and partly in the dream world. Dream insects scuttled around him in the darkness. He felt imprisoned by his paralyzed body on the floor. Words flowed through his mind, sayings which Manalk had often spoken to him but which were now uttered in the ajnir's sonorous, aged voice:

Suffering is evolution . . . through memory comes freedom.

As the dream continued, Nadan slowly became aware of a gentle but powerful presence standing over him. He didn't become fully aware of it until it was not more than an inch from his eyelids, mingling with his breath.

Nadan started from his dream. The strange insects, crawling along the walls, evaporated. His paralysis dissipated. And then the uriel was there, shimmering. In that instant, Nadan realized the being was somehow part of both the dream world and this world—but also separate and transcendent of either one.

He didn't have long to ponder this, however, because he now felt clearly the telepathing of the creature directly into his mind.

Planet traveler, it said.

There was a short pause. Then, it said:

To get to . . . become that world . . . unfolding . . . a mind.

Nadan's first instinct was to believe the uriel were just gibbers, as most scientists believed.

What the uriel said next, however, was a bit clearer:

Power from without . . . wind . . . wind retreats here and there . . . your world.

The writhing dialogue in his consciousness subsided. The being suddenly stood up in the air, its light-filled body pulsing in and out of Nadan's vision. Nadan thought it was about to depart, as it had done in Manalk's cave. But its luminescent arm came lashing down on top of Nadan, and he felt a ray of piercing, otherworldly energy vibrate through his being.

The being disappeared in the dark, like an extinguished flame. But Nadan felt the energy the being had sent him moving throughout his awareness, stretching to realms beyond thought. At that moment, with his growing telepathy, he felt the world about him in a more deep and profound way than he had ever felt before.

Before, with his evolving telepathy, Nadan had felt his mind stretching to areas around the city: the rivers in the mountains, the people on the streets in Simkada, the birds nesting in the nooks of trees. Now, he felt it expanding even further, to places he had never traveled. He felt the great city of Valyna, restless with ambitious energy, its people constantly seeking, competing, improving, inventing, controlling. Beyond it, over the never-ending sand of the Kiopic Desert, he felt the city of Kira Mandi, impoverished and windblown but holding a latent, mystical power.

He had always felt peace and serenity when he had stretched his mind into the environment. But now, he became aware of a different level to this reality, as his mind moved out deeper into the infinity of space beyond his body.

He felt reckless powers moving across the horizon: cities and people colliding, challenging one another in a quest for dominance. He felt great movement in the world beyond his quiet little city, beyond whose borders he had rarely ventured. The earth spoke of it; the sky told it in rumors. He felt at that moment a change in the air and soil, a change that would shake this world to its core. He felt terror and disaster, but he also felt new growth and life emerging from the rubble of death and decay.

Eventually, it grew to be too much. The world beyond and its complexities oppressed him. Sitting up, he proceeded to chant a meta, a mind-calming technique along his breath that Manalk had taught him. The phrase poured through his mind and soul, releasing the tension throughout his anxiety-stricken body. He went deeper and deeper into the song words, until the warlike world receded from his mind and, aloof and transcendent now, he became one with the essence of the chant.

At that same moment, Toruna was standing on the stone steps of his hut, a small crimson-domed dwelling near the western gates of the city. He had awoken in the middle of the night, an intense premonition blazing in his mind: *The arthanti is unsafe.* A month ago, Manalk had given it to him for safekeeping.

He had lain awake on his cool straw mat for a while before dressing, doubting his forethought, which he had never fully trusted. As he stood on the steps, Toruna now wrapped his golden cloak tighter around him in the chilly air, and the doubt resurfaced in his mind.

Perhaps it was just a dream, he wondered.

Slowly, Toruna made up his mind again and moved up the steps and through the moonlit glass doors of the crypt, where he served as chief of operations. He found the gem safe, in its usual location, lying quietly on the marble table in the room. It had not been moved or disturbed, and he remembered that a thin film of dust that he had noticed the day before still rested on the ancient ulten sphere, a form of rare metal that encased the stone.

He picked the case up in his hands and carried it awkwardly to the glass doors. When he reached the

The Ajnir

base of the steps, he placed the arthanti sphere down on the stone walkway for a moment to rest. At that moment, he heard footsteps along the walkway that circled the perimeter of the crypt. He sensed the thoughts of the men coming after him, and he felt their ill intentions sweeping toward him like a veil of black smoke. He picked up the gem, intending to flee. But, emerging from the tall, stately pafnegu trees at the corner of the walkway were several black-hooded shapes. Toruna started to run, his sandals clicking on the hard stone beneath his feet. He only got a few paces before he felt something strike him across the head.

In one instant before his eyes went dark, Toruna realized that he had responded to the premonition too late.

Chapter 5

A Journey Begins

The next day, Nadan returned to Manalk's cave but didn't find the old man there. Papers were swirling about inside the cave's back corners, near the old seer's gilded felmir desk. The floor of the cave had a large pile of dirt in it, as if someone had been digging beneath the floor. He searched for his master with his telepathy, but he received no response.

What happened here? he telepathed to Toruna. He was Manalk's closest friend, also an ajnir, and if anyone knew what had happened, it would be him.

I don't know, replied Toruna after a long pause, during which the breeze in the cave whispered in the cavities in the ceiling. *He may have left for Kira Mandi. He doesn't always tell people what he is doing.*

Toruna sounded complacent, and Nadan sensed he was busy reading over some manuscript in the crypt where he worked. Nadan used his remote viewing to scan the area where the old man was sitting. The circular room around him, its walls filled with paintings of ancient ajnir warriors, was in a state of disarray. Parchments and papers were scattered all over the room. A metallic green chair was turned over in the middle of the room, and a glass of water had spilled on the crimson rug, oozing beneath the low seat where Toruna was sitting. A stone pot of water was seething and humming on top of a small black electronic stove at the far edge of the chamber. Nadan noticed Toruna had a bandage wrapped around his head.

You are hurt, Nadan observed.

I fell last night. I have a concussion. Don't remember what happened.

Their conversation was interrupted by the maid-servant knocking on the door of Toruna's chamber. Toruna looked up, the white wrappings on his head swaying like a tiny tower. Nadan eyed the scene with his remote vision, which was unusually strong for some reason. He could hear the words coming from the two people's mouths with intense clarity. He wondered if this had to do with his experience with the uriel.

"Gahea," Toruna said. "Please put out the incense. It's going to make me cough."

The girl obeyed, kneeling down on the soft rug in front of the window and dabbing the incense out in her moistened fingers. Then she went to the stove and turned down the heat.

"Does your head still hurt?" she asked finally, standing up.

"Yes, it does some," said Toruna. "Thank you for asking."

The girl stretched out her hands, holding out two silver pills in her smooth brown palms. Nadan noticed her arm movements were sharp and poised, like Manalk's, moved as if by some fragile but power-fully subtle force. But he could tell she was irritated by his presence.

"These will ease the pain," she said.

Toruna thanked her but waved the pills off with his hand. Then he lay back on his cushion.

The girl suddenly became aware of Nadan, and for a second, he could see a tear forming along her eyelid. Then she left, her silver robe rustling slightly as she moved out of the door of the chamber.

Is she an ajnir? asked Nadan.

She was an orphan who awakened long ago, before I helped raise her.

She didn't seem to like me.

You looked like a boy she was in love with who hurt her feelings. You noticed she was crying a bit when she left. She wasn't sure if you were him at first. He was one of the strongest ajnir we had ever met in this city, but he left our world to join the army in Valyna. Many ajnir have renounced their awakening and drifted back to being regular common folk again. It has become an increasing problem in the last 70 years, and our numbers are dwindling.

"I don't understand why anyone would do that," Nadan said out loud, shaking his head.

There was a long pause in their talk, during which Nadan heard the rustling noise of anti-gravity skiffs skimming by on the street outside Toruna's room. Nadan wondered if it was the right time to ask the question burning in his mind.

You saw a uriel last night, Toruna telepathed finally, perceiving his question.

Not everything it said made perfect sense, but I could understand some things. I read once that the Wheel of Thought believe the uriel are deceivers. What do you think?

I'm not sure. Manalk told me when he first came to the city last summer that he had seen a uriel. He told me he had written down pages and pages of the being's words. He came to the belief that they were from one of the other multi-verses, perhaps the Dinjin, perhaps another dimension of which we know nothing, and that they were benign. The uriel said something about a great change on this planet.

"Manalk spoke of that change, when I first spoke to him," said Nadan, distantly. "Now, I have felt it, too." He said the words out loud, but he knew Toruna could hear him.

Toruna stared reflectively at the boy with his remote viewing for a second, then began massaging his wrists with his gnarled fingers. The pot on the electronic stove was still hissing and steaming, but the sound was slowly dying into silence.

I feel alarmed. Manalk is nowhere within my telepathic range. I fear the Order may have something to do with this.

So you don't know where he is?

The Wheel of Thought may have blocked us from speaking with him for some reason. He was never on good terms with Sakr Ka. Perhaps we'll find out soon enough.

Manalk had once told Nadan about Sakr Ka and his iron grip on the Wheel of Thought. Manalk said the numerous ordinances imposed by Sakr had steered him clear of the Wheel of Thought for years, but his master had told him little about the details of that relationship. Toruna, Nadan sensed, had regained his composure and seemed to be stewing over the words of the uriel.

You may consider doing what it said, the man telepathed finally.

"Going to Kira Mandi?"

Nadan's heart fluttered with a mixture of emotions. He had never journeyed outside his homeland, but he knew he would have to pass through Valyna to get to Kira Mandi. What he had heard and read about Valyna daunted him. Unfriendly people. Rampant politics and corruption. But also modernity and affluence. Yet the thought of going to Kira Mandi thrilled his mind.

"I don't have any money," protested Nadan.

I could lend you the money.

"But I don't even know what I'm supposed to do, once I get there."

Toruna curled his white moustache with his left index finger, then replied mysteriously, *The ajnir strive to act without strategy-filled motives.*

The ajnir seemed like he was going to explain the statement but instead became sunken in silence. Nadan felt his being absorbed into the man's quiet mood. Inner radiations emanated from his heart and mind and poured over into the atmosphere around him. Nadan felt himself being drawn deeper into the inner realms, until he found himself at the doorway of a reality he had only brushed with his mind in brief moments of meta-induced stillness.

Minutes of silence passed. Nadan and the ajnir still said nothing to each other.

~

And so the preparations began. Nadan planned to take few belongings with him. The great cargo road leading to Valyna was rarely traveled by Simkadans, and Toruna thought Nadan would probably have to travel on foot most of the way. Nadan didn't have enough money to buy an anti-gravity skiff, but he hoped they might get a ride with some of the cargo skiffs that occasionally traveled to the great metropolis during the summer months.

Nadan's family and friends, who thought his sudden decision to leave the city was rash, were for the most part disapproving of his plans to travel.

Historically, the two great cities of Simkada and Valyna had little to do with each other. Hundreds of years ago, the cities engaged each other in a fierce and extended war that had lasted decades. Just about everyone in the city had an ancestor who had died or been wounded in the war. Although the fighting eventually subsided into a general amnesty, emnity still existed between the peoples of both cities. Valynans were known to scoff at Simkadans as outlandish parvenus from the Old Order who shunned all forms of progress and technology. In turn, Simkadans had an innate suspicion about Valynans and their commercially oriented view of the world.

In recent years, however, the estrangement between the two cultures had begun to diminish ever so slightly, as trade between the two cities had begun to reemerge again. It wasn't common, but some Simkadan scholars, scientists, and political leaders had even begun traveling to Valyna, hoping to learn ways of improving the geopolitical or commercial operations of Simkada.

Though he could not disclose his secret reasons for going to Valyna to his relatives due to the ajnir secrecy code, Nadan came up with a different but equally true reason for going. "I won't be gone long," he told others. "I just feel a need to see Kira Mandi before I settle into my life here."

Meanwhile, Ranum was insistent that he go along, too. Initially, Nadan told him the uriel had specifically directed only him, not Ranum, to go to the city. But, then, the night before he was about to leave, Nadan was lying on his bed and saw an arm of light emerge from the crimson-colored clay wall of his kaaraadruun hut. The tiny cursive phosphorescent letters hovered for about a minute in the dark, amber room of his bedchamber before disappearing: *Your friend should go.*

Three nights later, when he was ready to depart, Nadan awoke Ranum in the early dawn, when the Light Star was just peeking above the perfectly flat line of horizon across the desert. He climbed the ladder onto the roof of Ranum's dome-hut and tapped his fingernails heavily on the glass. The clouded window, smeared with crimson dirt, creaked open after a few minutes. Ranum's eyes were bleary and fatigued.

"You can come," said Nadan. "The uriel told me tonight you must."

It took Ranum almost an hour to pack his belongings into a small woolen back pouch, but finally they were ready to leave. By that time, the sun was now gleaming off the roofs of the city and nomads were chanting their morning prayers in the streets, their voices rising and undulating in extended, vibrating waves above the city in the quiet morning air.

Together, they moved, speaking rarely to each other, through the streets toward the gates of Simkada. As they walked, Nadan felt a piercing sting of nostalgia move through his heart. He had often thought of leaving the city and setting out for Kira Mandi, but now that he was leaving, he felt an irrepressible sense of attachment to it. The cobblestones, the low, domed kaaraadruun huts, and the merchants' stands had never felt so inviting and comfortable. At the same time, his mind was moved with excitement, and not simply with the sort of anticipatory expectancy that many travelers experience. It was a deeper, soul excitement, as if with every step, he was breaking an invisible cord with his old ways, his old self-identity.

As they passed through the gates of the city, he felt a sort of vibrating energy, rippling in the sand and soil beneath his feet. He imagined for a moment the soil beneath him was alive, almost bursting out loud with a sudden wordless music.

"Did you feel that?" he asked Ranum, his toes still humming with the sensation.

Ranum was shielding his eyes in the sun, gazing at the road before them that led twisting and arcing up along the foot of the Thuresce Mountains to the east.

"Feel what?" replied Ranum, looking back with only vague interest.

"It felt like a slight tremor in the ground."

"Might have been a small earthquake," replied Ranum. "This area has been known to have seismic activity."

Together, they moved along the road. Neither of them had walked the road much before, but they soon found it was a more difficult task than they had imagined. The road was covered in fine dust that rose around them in small clouds as they walked. As the dust filled their nostrils and eyes, Nadan now understood why the Drogham nomads always had covered faces when they entered the city from abroad. He and Ranum tied shirts around their faces and continued walking up the road.

For hours, they trudged. They passed no one along the way except a ragged band of Drogham nomads who didn't speak Simkadan.

By midday, they had reached the shoulder of the mountain, where the Quantan Way, the central thoroughfare leading in and out of Simkada, veered back down toward a narrow strip of grass plains at the base of the mountains. From that elevated point, they could see the desert off to their side, like a seething, pale ocean, pockmarked with crimson, gray, and blue eddies and currents of different colored sand.

Valyna was still many miles away. Ranum, who had studied an electronic map before they left, suspected it would take almost a week to get there on foot.

As they moved along the shoulder of the mountain, a cargo skiff, a low red and black squarish vehicle, went skimming silently by them. Ranum tried to wave it down, but it never slowed. They kept walking. Nadan looked over his shoulder. Just over a mound of sand and a grassy knoll, Simkada's tentacle-like tunnels were disappearing from sight.

Will I ever see it again? he wondered.

The next moment, a violent wind whipped up from below the mountainside, and sand shrouded his last remaining view of the city. He could no longer see his homeland.

Nadan turned away and faced the downhill slope that led into Valyna. Neither he nor Ranum saw the small silver metallic orb that emerged from the sand where they had just been standing. The silver object hovered in the air for a moment before trailing them at a distance as they walked down into the plain below.

Chapter 6

Valyna

It took Nadan and Ranum more than a week to reach Valyna. On the third day, a sandstorm from the desert whipped across the Quantan Way, and they spent most of the day huddled under the lee of a massive rock with their spare robes tied around their heads. The fourth day was clear and the wind had calmed. They made progress, but the cargo skiffs that passed were still unwilling to take them to the city.

On the fifth day, thunderstorms arose from over the mountains to their left. They were fierce and violent squalls, so wild and furious that Ranum wasn't able to erect a small tent he had brought along for shelter. Fortunately, they had passed an encampment of Drogham just minutes before the storm struck. The nomads, hospitable but acquisitive, accepted them warmly and gave them food but wanted to trade all sorts of trinkets and gems with them.

It was the custom of guests among the Drogham to give gifts to their hosts after meals. Nadan parted with a woven cap he had brought along. Ranum gave the nomads one of his prized bead necklaces, which he had collected from Simkada's countless kiosks.

After the exchange, the leader, a small, irritable-looking man with large eyes and a crooked nose, spoke to them briefly. Nadan and Ranum sat opposite the man, named Valunx, a lumin-globe splattering fractured yellow light across the man's whiskered face. Outside, the wind howled sharply, ruffling the thick canvas of the pavilion. Nadan and Ranum both flinched, fearing it might collapse and blow off into the wind. The Drogham remained unmoved, his eyes glinting like a serpent's in the dark.

"The fighting has begun," the man muttered, stroking his beard thoughtfully. "We Drogham have no permanent home, so it makes us wonder and worry at times."

"What do you mean, darga?" asked Nadan, using the Drogham word for chief.

The Drogham chief stared at him moodily.

"Death, fire, breath," said the man, murmuring almost to himself. "I live in silence, until I break the shadows with my fist. The womb is near as the tomb. We march in silence."

"That's Yag, the Drogham poet," said Ranum.

"We always say that before a battle," said Valunx. "And tomorrow, we head to war alongside Simkada's finest soldiers."

"Against whom?" asked Nadan, with dismay filling his voice. Simkada hadn't waged war in almost a decade.

"Valyna, or had you not heard?" said Valunx.

"We had not," said Ranum.

"Simkada leaders had been keeping it secret until yesterday," said Valunx. "Simkada is all abuzz with the news now. The truce has broken. Valyna soldiers made a covert journey into the foothills of Zxe Mountain a few days ago. Simkada leaders are outraged and plan to retaliate with force."

Nadan and Ranum both stared at each other. Nadan was feeling upset that the departure of Manalk had spurred a war again between the two cities. On the ground around him, and in his homeland city beyond the whipping sand to the south, he could feel a deathly nightmare growing in the soil. He felt disturbed and shuddered, as he looked out through the entrance of the tent and into the storm.

Could it have been the soldiers in Manalk's cave? he asked Ranum, telepathically.

It must have been, replied Ranum. *Valyna soldiers haven't entered Simkadan territories in ten years.*

Valunx shook his head. "We have a contract with Simkada to help them in war, but many Drogham are upset with Simkada," he said, disappointedly. "But they are jumping into battle too quickly. None of those Valynan soldiers hurt or killed anyone. And now we are going to war again, over this trifle. Many of our men could die tomorrow. But Simkada will block off our trade routes if we break our agreement and don't come to their assistance."

"I don't know what to do," said Nadan, morosely. He was starting to feel depressed. He had often hoped that the war between Valyna and Simkada would end for good. And now with Manalk, his mind seemed to be moving within the nightmarish energy now permeating the desert.

Valunx threw some sand on the ground with his hand.

"Have you heard about the Anatami?" he asked, finally.

"The ancient tribe?" asked Nadan. "I thought they were extinct."

The primitive tribal nation had supposedly gone out of existence hundreds of years ago. It was said the tribe held the civilized world in contempt, roaming and living off the land without the aid of technology.

"No, no," said the man, his sandy voice bursting out with sudden animation. "They come back. We see them. Their heads with . . ."

The man paused, seeking for the words, rubbing his soiled fingers together in the air.

"Masks?" said Nadan.

"Yes, yes. We saw them after sandstorm. Way off. Deep into the sand." The man pointed across the Kiopic Desert with his pudgy index finger.

Nadan nodded, rubbing his chin with his fingers. He was skeptical of what the man said, but he had already seen things in the past few weeks that had fundamentally challenged the contemporary views of scientists. The uriel were real, he knew. Why couldn't an ancient, supposedly extinct tribe of Urshan Dai exist, too?

"Urum varana," the man said, reciting the Simkadan blessing. "I wish you the best in your travels." The man bowed low, his braided chin beard sweeping along the rug in the tent and whisking within centimeters of the lumin-globe. Then he turned and vanished into the storm toward his tent.

The rain and wind beat against Nadan's tent throughout the night. But in the early morning, the clouds broke and moved over the desert to the west. Ranum and Nadan continued trekking, after thanking the Drogham for their hospitality.

On the ninth day since their journey began, they were finally getting close to Valyna. That afternoon, Nadan first caught sight of the city. As they got closer, he could see the towers of the great city, glistening like translucent feathers on a monolithic swan. The transparent towers in the center of Valyna, bastions of the city's commercial pride, were a picture he had seen only in books before now. He had read that one could sit in the tall tiers of the towers and, from the highest floor, still see the street clearly below one's feet.

With the city in view, they stopped and rested on some ruby-colored rocks on the shoulder of the mountain. As he sat there sipping from his canteen, Nadan reviewed his training with Saaruun, much of which dealt with the art and science of accelerated self-adaption to unfamiliar conditions and climates. He remembered cold winter days, when Manalk had told him to spend the night with the Drogham, mixing as one of them in their tents outside Simkada. How the nomads had laughed at him at first, deriding the young Simkadan who had foolishly left his people! But by the next day, they had warmly accepted Nadan, almost as one of their own. The special meta phrase, spoken silently in the ancient ajnir tongue, had ultimately won them over. The phrase exerted special properties on the mind, making it pliable, dynamic, open to novelty and cultural nuance. It also made foreigners, even enemies, more receptive and inviting.

Although he had never been to a foreign city, Nadan felt his impending excitement at the idea melt in that same meta phrase, as he hummed it now silently to himself. He was so intent on the phrase that he failed to notice that Ranum had stood up and was eyeing him with a mystified expression.

"There's something I've been meaning to ask you," Ranum said.

"Yes," said Nadan, withdrawing his mind from the exercise.

"Manalk told me about this state of mind the ajnir call the Watching. I do not understand it. Manalk only spoke briefly of it before he left."

For a second, he looked at the ground, a reverential sadness playing across his face.

"He said it has to do with knowing things directly," Ranum said, completing his thought. "Do you know what this is?"

"Manalk once told me that people assume they don't know the answers to things, but in fact, the answers are already inside of them," said Nadan. "Scientists, for example, always look to outward experience to learn. Manalk said that is a slower way to learn; most people do not open themselves to the notion that their minds are already imbedded with the answers. Later, experience and experiment can ratify what is learned from the Watching."

Ranum said nothing for a moment and looked wistfully to the city of Valyna, resting like a distant ice sculpture amidst the skirting traces of red and black sand.

"And what does the Watching tell you now?" he said, at length. "What will we find here, other than mockery, imprisonment, or death?" His last word fell like a heavy note in the air, which seemed to mingle and drift away with the sand.

"I cannot say what we will find," said Nadan, after a pause. "I do not have the skill in tapping the Watching enough. But I do not think the uriel or Toruna would have told us to go here if we were to die."

Their conversation ended, and they began walking again. Over the mountain, storms rumbled and thundered but did not threaten them. They had been walking another few hours when they both caught the scent of a smell that was salty and cooly revitalizing to their senses.

"What is that?" Nadan asked.

"It is the smell of the Arwanu Sea, I think," said Ranum.

Nadan had read many times of the great ocean of Arwanu, which stretched out along the shores of the planet's great metropolis, Valyna. He wanted to see the vast expanse of water, but their line of sight was blocked by a formless mist enshrouding the city.

"It is strange," said Ranum. "It feels like I've smelled it before, as if in a dream I once had that I am now remembering."

Nadan said nothing and squinted through the brilliant sunlight toward Valyna's gates. At that moment, he noticed two small anti-gravity skiffs moving along the road toward them from the city gates. They were approaching rapidly. Their silvery sides seemed to wiggle like fish in the heat waves.

"Look," Ranum said, grabbing hold of Nadan's robe.

The skiffs were moving toward them even more quickly now. As soon as Nadan looked up, they were almost upon them. There were red shapes on top of them, and on their heads were the familiar beast-like masks he remembered seeing not too long ago. For a second, his mind raced: What if Sakr Ka had sent the Valynan warriors to intercept him? He looked around the rocks for an instant but saw no escape. The rock wall to their left was sheer and unscalable.

The warriors were now moving past them, showing the common courtesy of slowing down while passing pedestrians along the road. Nadan exhaled slightly, as they moved on past, their heads nodding in synchrony with the vertical movement of their crafts. One of them turned his head to glance at Ranum from under his ugly beast mask, molded in the shape of a gargoyle. He veered his skiff away from the road, and with a wave of his red glove, motioned his comrade onwards, as he circled around and parked his skiff near Ranum and Nadan. Nadan's heart began racing in his chest. He stretched his mind to feel what was happening in the man's mind, but as before, when he was drugged in Manalk's cave, he could discern no details about the man's mind.

The man lifted up his mask on his forehead, exposing a rugged, young, handsome face, with a lean, muscular jaw. His cheeks were unshaven, and black stubble stretched all along his lower left jaw. A braided rope of hair curled out of his helmet, snaking along his red armored breastplate.

"You are Simkadans, aren't you?" he asked. "We don't see many of you people along this road, and when we do, they are mainly adults."

He eyed them suspiciously, and Ranum shifted uncomfortably. At that moment, a gust of wind swept up and blew sand across the man's face, and he quickly closed his face guard to protect himself from the blast.

"We are coming to Valyna only for a short while," said Ranum, finally speaking up. "We plan to journey to Kira Mandi afterward. We want to see the Great Fault before we are both married and have too much to do with our lives."

"Kira Mandi," the warrior repeated. "We have had a truce with them now, but the agreement is fragile. Do you know what I am doing on this road today?"

Ranum shook his head. The man looked at him severely, as he raised the mask on his forehead again.

"We are looking for Simkadan spies," he said. "There have been reports of them in the city recently, and we cannot be too careful. The Anatami Road, which leads to Kira Mandi, is more heavily guarded, but we are also patrolling this road, more to prevent spies from entering from the south, after the treaty with Simkada was broken. Your faces are white, and you speak like Simkadans, as you say. You are still young, which makes me wonder if you are really spies. But the Simkadans have always been the most cunning in their war strategy."

The man took a sip from the canteen bottle at his chest. Then, he began talking into his wrist, where Valynan warriors carried a telecommunication device to speak with their comrades and officers.

He's going to imprison us and take us in for questioning, telepathed Ranum to Nadan, anxiously.

He must be with Sakr Ka. I can feel it, for some reason, replied Nadan.

Nadan scanned the cliffs around them. They were unscalable, but there was a small slit in the cliff to the south several feet away which looked large enough for their bodies. Where the opening in the cliff went, it was impossible to tell. But Nadan felt it was their only chance, and Ranum concurred telepathically.

Meanwhile, the warrior stopped talking on his telecom device and was now eyeing the two boys' bags and clothes with disgust.

"Do you have a passport?" he asked.

"No," said Nadan. "What is that?"

"It is a new rule in the city, since the spies began infiltrating our army," the man replied. "No foreigners are allowed into the city without a passport and prior clearance from our army's chief officers. That is the only way I could let you into the city. If you don't have one, I'll have to chain you and bring you to my commander."

The man pulled his mask down over his face again, as the wind and sand swept across the desert. Nadan and Ranum both knew the momentary diversion was perhaps their only chance. Ranum had understood already what Nadan was planning and had already taken a few steps back along the road. At the same exact second, they pivoted on their heels and began running as fast as they could. But the warrior, whose name was Dargon, was no fool. He had risen through the command of his army in a matter of a few years, when many his age were still at the lowest rank of dwisnas. Even as the boys turned, he pulled his gun from his shoulder and shot a stun arrow into Nadan's left leg. Ranum, who was quicker and more athletic than his friend, was able to scramble off behind a rock beside the road before the man could get another shot off. Then, he darted into the entrance at the edge of the cliff and into the rock wall.

Dargon began speaking into his telecom device in his glove.

Nadan was paralyzed from the waist down. His legs were cold and numb, but he could still weakly move his fingers and hands slightly, as the drug took control of his body. It felt very similar to the night when he had been injected with the drug during Manalk's kidnapping. But this time, he didn't feel himself losing consciousness.

The warrior now bent over him, pushing his fingers into the bag at his shoulder.

"Who are you?" he asked, taking one of his gloves off.

Nadan remained silent.

The man sighed and began cuffing his legs with two silver chink chains around his feet. But even as he did, the man froze, paralyzed, it seemed; his face abruptly turned to the color of white ash, Nadan could see. After a few seconds, he fell over, slouching to the sand. Ranum emerged from behind the rock and began cutting loose the silver chains on Nadan's feet.

"What did you do?" asked Nadan.

"Combat meta," said Ranum. "Manalk did not want to teach those techniques to me at first. But finally, he agreed. I'm glad he did, in retrospect . . ."

Nadan got to his feet and looked at the warrior. A bead of sweat was dripping from his forehead, and drool was draining from the left side of his mouth. Nadan's feet were wobbly from the drug dart, but he was quickly recovering.

"Will he die?"

"No," said Ranum, lifting the man's mask off his face. "It's a paralysis meta. He'll wake out of it in a few gyras. He probably won't remember what just happened, so I doubt he will report us. We'll have to hurry."

Nadan took the mask from Ranum and turned it over in his hands. Inside, he could see a lining of some fabric, like very soft silk. He pulled it out and looked at it closely. "I wonder if this is what repels telepathing," he said. He put the fabric on his head for a second, and asked Ranum to read his thoughts. His friend couldn't.

"This is just what we may need in the city," Ranum said. "There are so many ajnir in Valyna, and many of them are in league with Sakr Ka. I think it's large enough that we can cut it in half and put it inside our hoods. We'll have to use concealing metas when our hoods aren't on."

Taking one more look at the man paralyzed in the sand, they moved down the dusty road toward the city. In a few minutes, they were at the great silver gates, which reared up magnificently above the desert landscape. They paused before the gates, at the edge of the road, while Ranum quickly fitted the stolen linen they had confiscated from the soldier into each of their hoods, just below the fabric line. No one, except the Valynan warriors, had exited through the city's gates since Ranum and Nadan had begun their walk down toward the city. But as they started walking again and drew near, a line of anti-gravity skiffs zoomed out of the gates and dispersed in different directions, most toward the western desert.

Ranum and Nadan reached the gates and walked through their silvery, tall arches. They found themselves in a bustling square with smooth gray sandstones and high-roofed kaaraadruun huts. As in Simkada, the Drogham merchants had set up their markets just inside the gates, and their familiar, deep-throated accents were the first sounds that met their ears. In front of the huts, Valynans were walking and standing, chattering and yelling and laughing. Pale-skinned and tall, they were dressed in strange but elegant robes, patterned with zigzagging lines and symbols. As they walked closer, Nadan could see that many of the Valynans had glinting rings on their fingers and enormous medallions that few Simkadans, who tended to be frugal and less gaudy, would wear or be able to afford.

As he looked at them closely, Nadan thought their faces and body motions seemed almost animalistic. But from that very first moment, Nadan was attracted to them. The men wore proud, deep smiles and long, braided chin beards that fell to their stomachs. The women looked sophisticated and wore intricate webs of exotic gems and studded necklaces around their heads and necks. The sounds of laughter echoed off the stones in the courtyard. Nadan could immediately sense an outgoing quality to the people.

With his growing ajnir telepathy, Nadan stretched his mind around the city for a moment. The first sensations he noticed in the minds of the people around him were of extroversion, rushing, and aggression. He looked closely around the square where he was walking; the impression was reinforced. The square was thronging with more people than anyone would ever see inside Simkada, even during the most popular holidays. Valynans were moving about hastily, holding up coins between their fingers over the heads of others, while Drogham haggled with them over prices for jewelry or other wares displayed on tables on the street.

Together, Nadan and Ranum pushed their way through the crowd. In one sense, they found that the concealing meta phrases actually gave them a disadvantage: people were less aware of them, and they often found people stepping on their toes or nearly pushing them to the ground as they pushed their way through. Eventually, after much pushing and shoving, they came out on the other side, where a wide cobblestone street led toward the center of the city.

The street was less crowded than the square at the gates, but they were confronted with numerous anti-gravity skiffs that darted quickly along the thoroughfare. Nadan noticed that the kaaraadruun huts that bordered the street were higher and more stately than the ones in Simkada. Many had massive, hanging Valynan flags flailing in the breeze and great balconies, littered with tall trees and colorful floral displays. They kept walking down the road. Suddenly, Ranum halted, his neck craning up at a sign above a massive kaaraadruun hut that stretched for hundreds of feet along the street.

"Look," he said, pointing.

Nadan gazed upward. A weather-beaten granite stone, inscribed with deep black runes, creaked on metallic hinges over a black door. The runes spelled the words "Quenna Corporation."

Manalk had told them that the Quenna Corporation was the name for the Wheel of Thought's central headquarters, where a secret labyrinthine mine lay beneath the building. Nadan immediately sensed the energy surrounding the place, subtle electrical impulses that emanated as if some ecstatic level of ground lay beneath them.

Nadan looked at Ranum, and they both knew immediately what the other felt. Spells and ajnir phrases wove around the place, keeping it subtly camouflaged to eyes which daily intruded upon it. But there was more to it than that. Nadan sensed the nexus of inner power and recycled heritage that had breathed new life into the ancient, interconnected seer lineage for millennia. A word came into his mind at that moment, from the ancient ajnir tongue: *kayom*. It meant home.

"Should we go in?" asked Ranum, staring at the door skeptically. "I don't sense that all the ajnir here can be as bad as Sakr Ka."

Nadan could tell that his friend also sensed the strange magnetism from the place but shook his head doubtfully. As much as he wanted to meet other ajnir, he knew they needed to mask their presence in the city. The image of Sakr Ka's torpid, overpowering eyes still stung his mind.

Toruna had spoken to him before he left of Sakr Ka's obsession with prophecy and prediction. Hadn't that strange comment come true? Did the uriel want him to visit Sakr Ka in Valyna?

Nadan searched his mind, attempting to deepen his still-developing awareness into the Watching. *No*, he thought finally, *the uriel would not want me to.*

Ranum was running his fingers along the wall of the kaaraadruun hut, his face lit with a mystical pleasure. Nadan came over and grabbed his wrist softly. "No, I do not think we should go here," he said, quietly. "Not yet, at least."

Reluctantly, Ranum pulled his hand from the crimson, mud-caked wall. "All right," he said, looking longingly at the place. "Sakr Ka would probably know. But you know this place looks familiar."

For a moment, Nadan was reminded of his dreams of Kira Mandi in childhood and how many times he had walked its crowded streets, though he had never been there. But he did not share the thought or the dreams out loud with Ranum.

That night, they slept in an inn not far from the Quenna Corporation. Toruna had given them a large sum of money: 100,000 cagmas, but they realized quickly that they had to be cautious in their spending. Valyna was much more expensive than Simkada, and the first night alone cost them more than a week in a Simkadan inn.

The next day, Nadan went to the transportation center for the city. After the uriel had told him to go to Kira Mandi, he had assumed Valyna was the best way to reach Kira Mandi from Simkada. Simkada was at the farthest point on the planet away from Kira Mandi, and the Kiopic Desert stretched for thousands of miles between the two cities. No significant trade could ever exist between the cities quite simply because the desert was too long a journey for any anti-gravity skiff without refueling, and no trade routes had ever been established between the two cities.

Nadan had hoped that there might be cargo skiffs or perhaps even a transit service that shuttled between Valyna and Kira Mandi. But there he learned, much to his disappointment, that the only way to reach Kira Mandi from Valyna was to buy an anti-gravity skiff and navigate it across the desert on his own. His heart fell at once when he heard the news. How would he ever raise the money to buy a luxury that only the wealthiest in Simkada could afford?

But that day, as he walked back to the inn, he saw an ad, nailed to a wooden post along one of the city's gardens. It read: "Workers needed. Pays well, almost a magistrate's salary. Intercom Annod at TGREC."

Nadan dialed the code on the transportation center's intercom. A man answered with a gruff accent he had never heard before. It was nothing like the smooth, polished accent of the Valynans he had heard so far. This was like hard stone and dirt and kaaraadruun mud all mixed together.

"Come see me tomorrow morning," the man said, bluntly. The man was about to cut off the intercom, but Nadan interrupted him.

"What kind of work is it?" he asked.

"Acron mining," the man said. "It's not exciting, but it pays a magistrate's salary."

There was a sound of gases steaming and metals grating together in the background, and Nadan lost the rest of what the man was saying. The man cut his intercom off.

Nadan walked back to the inn, thinking: *This might be our only way to reach Kira Mandi.* Even the cheapest anti-gravity skiffs cost 500,000 cagmas, he knew. Toruna had given them only 100,000. Working in Simkada, 100,000 would take him at least a year to make.

When he got back to the inn, Ranum was already there. He had been visiting the city's wharfs that stretched all along the seashore of Valyna, and his eyes were glowing with a warmth Nadan hadn't seen on his friend's face in years. Nadan could tell immediately his friend was more drawn to the city than he was.

The next day, they set out for the acron mine, where the man had told Nadan to meet him. The mine was on the outskirts of the city, a pitch-black hole set inside the center of a small hill with paf-negu trees and a winding stone path leading up its dented silver metal door. Outside was the head-quarters, a small, white, nondescript hut with a sign over the doorway that read: "Annod's Mining Corp."

Inside, they found Annod himself, sitting at a table and talking furiously on an intercom. Nadan at once recognized the same gravelly voice he had heard over the intercom, but he had pictured a larger, more imposing man. Annod was slim, and although his voice was rough as before, he was well dressed. He wore a long, black robe with silver sym-bols woven into it and a gilded turban that virtually all Valynans wore when they worked. His face was smooth-shaven, and his eyes were hazel, hungry, and flitting from side to side. His wide jowls, flexing as he spoke, reminded Nadan of fighting dogs he used to see in the streets of Simkada.

The man was leaning back in his chair, feet upon the table. Around the room were scattered papers, a number of shovels, and an amber lumin-globe that blinked on and off every few minutes. Ranum and Nadan sat down on the metal settee at the right of Annod's desk.

Eventually, the man shut off his intercom.

"You must be Nadan," he said, not even pausing for a moment.

"Yes. And this is Ranum," said Nadan.

Stepping out from behind the table, the man bowed roughly in the fashion of Valynans, a quick high bend without any pause. Nadan and Ranum both did so also, but somewhat awkwardly, since this was the first time they were attempting the custom.

The man rubbed his smooth face with his soiled fingers.

"Simkadans, eh?" he asked.

"Yes." said Nadan.

"You aren't scientists, are you?"

"No, we're traveling through Valyna, so that we can get to Kira Mandi. I need to purchase a skiff to get there."

The man looked at them both distrustfully for a moment. For an instant, Nadan wondered if he had made a mistake telling the man he wanted to go to Kira Mandi. Valynans, he knew, held even greater animosity toward Mandians than their dislike for Simkadans.

"What do you want to do there?" the man asked, masking his disgust slightly.

The tone of his voice was half curious, half accusing.

"We want to see the Great Fault, the Gortag."

"A skiff is quite a price to pay for a view," said Annod, with mild interest. "But it's a sight to behold, I'll grant that."

The man seemed to lose interest in the subject immediately. He slid his hand across the desk, sending a few small papers to the floor. He ignored them, drawing out a different set of papers from a small drawer inside his desk.

"These are the contracts," he said. "I'll need you to sign them, for legal reasons, of course. And then we'll set you to work right away."

"How much does the job pay?" asked Nadan.

"500,000 cagmas per year."

Nadan and Ranum both looked at each other. This was as much money as the most affluent in Simkada made. For a second, Nadan wondered: *Why is this work so easy to obtain?* But something held him from putting the question directly to the man.

After they had signed the papers, Nadan and Ranum followed Annod into the mine itself through a round, rusted metal door at the other side of the hut. The smell of salt and steam stung their nostrils immediately, as they walked down a narrow stairway and into a black cavern where pistons heaved and black steam billowed out long tubes that stretched out along the side of the hill. Men with dark, sooty faces and glittering eyes shifted to and fro along a metal track, carrying huge leather baskets and dumping their contents onto a conveyor belt that coursed through the center of the mine. At the back of the mine, Nadan could see a huge, cavernous shaft. Out of it was pouring a steady stream of small cylindrical carts on a silver conveyor belt. A trail of smoke or steam was jetting out of the shaft and disappearing into the black nothingness, the cave's ceiling.

Nadan was so intent on watching the conveyor belt, he didn't notice that Annod was standing right next to him with one of the small cylinders gripped in his right arm.

"These carry the soil up to this area, where the men sift through it by hand," he noted, holding the cylinder so Nadan could see through the end of it.

A short, pallid-skinned man next to Annod handed him a small device with a large screen connected to it.

"You unscrew the cylinder, like this," Annod said, turning the black cap of the cylinder. "Then we attach the screen to the end and dump all the soil through it."

With a sharp flick of his arm, Annod turned the cylinder over, and the soil fell out of it, like a brown river, into a white mat at his feet. Then, he turned it over again and removed the screen, holding it for Ranum and Nadan to see. The screen was full of glinting green and peridot-colored stones, ranging from the size of a marble to a pebble of sand. Annod reached into his robe, pulling out some telescoping glasses. He held up a large nugget from the screen, zeroing in the lens on the stone.

"This is fairly pure," he said, squinting in the lumin-globe over his head. "Perhaps 35 caloa. But you don't need to worry about quality. That's the task of the examiners."

Annod took off the telescoping glasses and, placing the stone on the screen, walked over and dumped its contents into a small shaft inside a large silver machine over against the charcoal-and-lavender-colored rock wall. The machine made a gentle slurping sound, then became quiet again.

"That's all you have to do," said Annod, turning to face them. "If you learn to spot a good rock, we may make you an examiner. But it will take months before you can do that. When I have time, I will show you how to do it, if you like. Any questions?"

Nadan and Ranum both shook their heads.

"Very well, then," said Annod, with a pat of his pale hand on Ranum's shoulder. "I will be up in my quarters if you have any questions."

Annod turned and went up the stone staircase that they had just come down. The small man gave them a coerced smile before following him up the stone staircase. Nadan and Ranum immediately set about their work, taking the cylinders off the conveyor belt, unscrewing them, and then sifting the green acron into the silver machine.

The other miners mostly ignored them for the first hour, but Nadan silently kept saying the meta phrase in his mind, the one that stimulated openness and trust. He knew these men were suspicious of foreigners. He didn't need his telepathy to perceive it, but still, he could feel the xenophobia radiating out from the thoughts of the men like a chill, icy air. After a time, the meta phrase became more powerful; it flowed through his being, emanating into the corners of the cave. Finally, a heavyset man, dressed in nothing but a red loincloth, came over.

"Those beads are from Simkada," the man said, pointing to the necklace on Ranum's neck. "Where did you buy those?"

He had a different accent than Annod, Nadan noticed. It was thicker, rougher, and more difficult to understand.

"Simkada," said Ranum, taking the necklace off. "The nomads there sell these necklaces everywhere. You can have it if you like."

Jagar wiped his face with a towel and let his brown fingers slide along the necklace. The machine next to them groaned for a second, then went silent.

"I can pay you for it," he said. "How about four?"

"Five," said Ranum.

"You're like one of those Drogham hagglers," said Jagar, with a wave of his hand.

"Well, that's what I paid for it in Simkada."

"Ah," said Jagar. "No war words between us."

The man smiled and whipped out five clear, freshly minted coins from the leather pocket on his thigh. As he was handing them to Ranum, another miner, in a black robe like Annod's, came up and tapped Jagar on the shoulder. The man's sallow face was grim and serious, and for a few moments, he and Jagar moved off and whispered together in a hushed, serious tone. Then, the man's form melted into the shadows, and Jagar came back. Ranum handed him the bead necklace.

"They pay well here," Nadan said.

"Not many into it, though," said Jagar.

"Why not?"

"Not Eroni," the man retorted, with a look of contempt on his face. "Hate 'em all, the way they stride around, like that. Not for me, I say."

Then, Nadan remembered. Eroni were the educated class of Valyna, while the Zaltin, such as miners, were a working-class demographic. He recalled reading in history books in Simkadan's crypts once years ago about the sharp lines of class distinction in Valyna. But lately, the barricades between the two societal strains had been softening. It had been once inconceivable for a Zaltin to become Eronin. A newer generation of Valynars had begun changing that, with some natural-born Zaltins becoming Eronins.

Jagar wiped his chest with the towel and placed it back on the top of the machine, then pulled out a handful of acron from the pocket at his thigh. He moved over to the machine, dumping it into the tray, and flushed it into the processor. The machine whirred and then came to a stop.

Jagar returned to his seat and opened another cylinder, which he had taken off the conveyor belt.

"Many miners are gettin' to be busy Eroni folk in the city," he said. "We call him busy people. That work is getting better, I say and everyone says. Why Annod was so quick to hire you. All 'em here are leaving to become busy."

It finally made sense to Nadan. Annod was desperate for workers. He and Ranum had both said the meta phrase to elicit Annod's trust, but even with that, Nadan had wondered why he was so willing to sign two foreign outsiders as workers and why he was willing to pay so much.

Throughout the course of the afternoon, Nadan and Ranum both got to know the other workers. Many had eyed them skeptically at first, but Nadan had kept uttering the special meta phrase as he continued to work. Slowly, the men warmed to him, and by the end of the day, they were talking freely with him, as if they had known each other for years.

With more cagmas in their pockets than they had ever seen, Ranum and Nadan were able to rent a small kaaraadruun hut in the center of Valyna after a few weeks. On their days off, they would enjoy some of their newfound money, taking rides in the long-skiff ships that took frequent trips across the Arwanu Sea or touring the city's great towers and temples. They ate well, dining at new inns almost nightly and trying out new foods and restaurants in Valyna. But always Nadan was cautioning Ranum to check his spending, knowing that they had to reserve most of their money for their journey to Kira Mandi.

The days flew by pleasantly. Valyna had a warmer climate than Simkada, and the winters in the city were as cool and refreshing as summer evenings in Simkada. But as the days wore on, Nadan soon began to wonder about his mission and why the uriel had brought him to this place. Was it simply to enjoy a new culture? Or did the being want him to go to Kira Mandi as swiftly as possible? He felt his greater purpose lay there, but he couldn't escape the notion that the uriel wanted something achieved in Valyna. Sometimes, in the dark hours of the night, Nadan would reach out telepathically, trying to attract the being back to him. But the luminous entity never returned, even if he called out to it urgently. At times, he would also stretch out his mind to Toruna, but an enigmatic silence seemed to hang around the other ajnir's mind like a thin, ethereal veil, making it impervious to Nadan's psychic abilities.

The days grew into months, but still Nadan had no answer, nor another visitation from the uriel.

The summer turned into autumn, then into winter, which was cold at night but comfortably chilly during the daytime. It was during this time that Annod hired a man from Kira Mandi at the mine. It was a shocking move, but Annod was short on miners. The two cities had been at war for decades, and now Annod was hiring one of them, one of the enemy, in his own mine. The move outraged many of the men; many grumbled about it among themselves, but none dared challenge Annod directly.

The Mandian was dark skinned and slight of build, with a short dirty white cloth tied around his hips. He had a long chin like an antelope. He had a crescent-moon tattoo on his left shoulder, emblazoned in black, and a large gold earring stuck in his left ear. When he talked to people, he would stare at them deeply for several seconds before answering. He wore nothing but a Mandian sitosis, and he had an aura of poverty about him, a fact which hardly surprised Nadan, knowing what he had read about the rampant poverty in Kira Mandi. But the man had that mysterious peacefulness in his expression which Nadan had noticed suffused the faces of many Mandians whom he had seen in paintings and photographs. It was, perhaps, a universal trait in that race, he thought, just as most Simkadans exuded a feeling of ancient intelligence.

Nadan was instantly drawn to him, partially because of that expression, but also because he had, with the exception of Saaruun, rarely ever spoken with a Mandian. He questioned the man, whose name was Ternaz, many times about Kira Mandi. He asked him to describe the Great Fault in detail: the streets, the people, the temples, the kiosks which Nadan had seen clearly in his dreams.

The Valynan miners were far less enthused about their new colleague. None of them went over to welcome Ternaz; instead, they remained separate and apart from the Mandian all day, glancing over now and then distrustfully, their eyes glittering in the gloom of the cave. Nadan knew that many of the miners had lost relatives in the Mandian War, and the pain of their grief was still near the surface of their emotions. Jagar himself had lost an uncle in a battle on the Kiopic Desert only two years before.

Nadan was sitting on the black mound of dirt, sewing a patch onto his leather acron pouch, when hostilities finally erupted a few days later. Huddled in a circle outside the inlet of darkness that led deep into the acron cavern, Jagar and two other miners, Gaf and Draqu, were eating some whey bread. Teranun, a crippled old Valynan, sat nearby in a crouch, back hunched, sifting soil through his fingers and digging with a small shovel.

The miners were speaking rapidly in Valynan, the strange language rising and falling like bubbles of foam in the air. Nadan was listening intently. He knew some of the words in the language, and he was already learning how to speak haltingly in the strange speech, but the men's verbal exchanges were so fast it was mostly unintelligible to him. He caught different words drifting into his ears, up into the stifling air of the cavern. One stung the air suddenly like venom: *radi*. Nadan wasn't certain what the term meant, but he could feel its effect, in the air, like a red serpent stinging the vibrations in the cavern. Their eyes flitted over to the Mandian, crouched on the floor. A derisive laugh rose and fell quickly in the air.

Nadan leaned closer to Ranum, who was next to him stirring his finger in the sand at the moment.

What does radi mean? he telepathed.

Ranum kept stirring the sand with his finger and didn't respond at first. He was too intent on watching the Mandian, who was sitting over against the machine, scratching his bare left shoulder. Nadan looked over at the man. His face seemed unperturbed, tranquil. He was not letting his attackers see his wound, but Nadan could sense it there, deeply.

Not a nice term for Mandians, replied Ranum, who knew the Valynan language a bit better.

Jagar and the others were now laughing and talking loudly again, as if nothing had transpired. The Mandian Ternaz stood up, and the three miners fell silent again, awaiting his response. Nadan sensed a transparent thread of hostility stretching between them. For a moment, with some deeper visionary faculty, he saw the people in front of him as small vortexes, swirling around invisible axes in their spinal columns. Each of the vortexes was gravitating toward the others, but there was one that was repelling them, deflecting the energy of the other vortexes, like a whirlpool pushing water away from itself. The vision faded quickly, and Nadan found himself sitting on the ground where he was, the same hostility moving, shifting, like tense waves in the air. The physical shapes of the men were there before him again but still faintly luminous with the subtle energy of the vortexes he had seen in the vision state. After a few more moments, Ternaz gathered up his few belongings—a dusty brown turban and a red clay cup—and walked out of the cave. Nadan felt as if centuries of malice were radiating from Ternaz's expression. He took one more glance around the cave, before walking slowly out into the dull mist shrouding the entrance of the cave. His hostile vibration seemed to silence the crowd of workers, who stood there fidgeting for a moment with their turbans. As soon as he was gone, the silence snapped palpably in the air, and the miners began talking all at once.

Even as their voices started again, Nadan felt wrath boiling in his veins, a powerful, righteous anger that had seethed in him at various times throughout his life. But he checked himself quickly, soothing his mind with a quieting meta Manalk had taught him. Later that night, he probed the Watching, lying on the floor in his kaaraadruun hut, stirring his hand through the sand floor of his hut. Long hours passed. Morning arrived, banishing the shadows of his chamber. With it came an idea, as if formed by silent fingers from another world.

He got up immediately and went out to the kiosk outside his hut. There was a Drogham woman there, with long black braids that fell to her feet. She was shouting in Valynan at the people moving along the street like a restless, chaotic stream.

"I'm looking for a sitosis," he announced, in a quiet voice.

The woman stopped her shouting.

"You a Mandian, with that pale skin?" she said, turned, snorting a laugh.

"I just want it," he said.

The woman looked at him again, this time more seriously. Nadan couldn't tell whether her shrewd brown eyes were still deriding him.

"Let me look around," she said, finally. "I may have one. Wait here."

A few minutes later, she came out holding a small sitosis, a Mandian cloak, in her arms. Nadan gave her 40 cagmas for it. He also purchased an Eroni robe, with an elegantly shaped dragon embossed in gold silk on the surface. It cost him substantially more, a total of 300 cagmas. Then, he bought a Zaltin robe for 125 cagmas.

"It's a bit early for the Nagchan Festival," said the woman. It was a festival in the early spring, when people would parade around in costumes, similar to Simkadan's Urum Festival, and dance all night into the morning.

Nadan frowned and returned to his hut, where he took the sitosis, threw it into some mud, then hung it up on a line inside his hut to dry.

The next day, he wore the Eroni robe to the mine. The men all started laughing at once when they saw him, but Nadan neither smiled nor frowned. He looked at them with such silence and solemness that some of them even stopped and stared, even with respect. Overnight, Nadan had transformed himself into the image of a wealthy man, and he played the part well. He walked with each foot falling directly in front of the other, as he had observed for months, sitting and watching the Valynans' wealthy men parade by him on his days off. He would lift his robe up when he walked and let it drop again as he stood still.

The men would start laughing again, when he talked like that, but he kept doing it, until some of them turned and talked to one another. Nadan could sense their conversation as they walked away:

"*He's lost his mind,*" said one.

"*He is a Simkadan, and they are strange folk,*" said another.

"*Too much clinus for him,*" laughed another.

The next day, Nadan dressed as a miner, wearing the black pants and the turban and play-acting as a member of the Valynan underclass. The effect was similar. Many laughed; others shook their heads as he walked by. But increasingly they were becoming interested in what Nadan was doing, and talk was buzzing around the mine about it. Again, Nadan sensed their thoughts after he had left that day. But by the end of the day, some were trying to oust him from the mine completely.

"*Someone should tell Annod about this,*" he heard Ternanun tell one man. "*The boy is too strange.*"

On the third day, Nadan wore the sitosis. It was black and stained and worn by now, just like the ones worn by Mandians. He went to the mine shirtless and worked all day, speaking with a Mandian accent. He found this role simpler than his two previous ones. After spending so much time listening to Saaruun, who spoke with a Mandian accent, he found the speech characteristics and inflections to be almost second nature, innate to his understanding. But he almost thought it was something deeper than that, something more primordial than he had imagined, almost as if he was recollecting a long lost memory that he had entirely forgotten. And yet, as he thought about it, he couldn't understand why he had this intuition or what its significance was.

In the middle of the afternoon, Jagar walked slowly up to Nadan, sitting down next to him on the red embankment on the edge of the cave's glittering walls. His turban had slumped off his head, angling at the ground, and he was sweating heavily. Nadan noticed his eyes were reflective, almost dull with a sort of psychological weariness that transcended any amount of physical fatigue.

"I think I know this thing you do," he said, taking his turban off for a moment and wiping it with his hand. "But we do not feel regret for what we have said."

Nadan said nothing but kept sifting the dirt thoughtfully with his hands. This was going just as he had planned.

"The Mandians are the ones who started this war, so why should I like any of them?" Jagar continued. His voice was now fraught with lines of wrath, years of torment and grief that Nadan could sense emanated from the deeper, unspoken realms of this city's collective mind.

"They killed my uncle, and they killed many more of our folk," he went on, his voice intensifying. "Mandians hate us, and we hate them. It will always be that way, at least for our generation."

Nadan let some slip through his fingers and watched the remaining acron glinting greenish-black in his wet palm. Finally, he looked over at Jagar, slowly and steadily, meeting the man's washed-out eyes, reddish-tinged pools of black glowing in the light of the lumin-globe overhead.

"I am not trying to make you feel regret," he said, finally.

A slight line of anger crossed Jagar's sooted face.

"Then what are you doing, young one?" he asked, in a low, harsh voice.

Nadan smiled as he stirred the sand with his index finger, but said nothing.

Chapter 7

The Wheel of Thought

The next day, Annod's head servant came down to the acron cave and came to a halt halfway down the stone stairs, while Nadan was sitting next to the acron machine, feeling its pulsing engine massage his back.

"My master wants to see you," said the servant, calmly.

The man's voice was objective and detached, as if merely performing a duty. Nadan sensed he didn't know what this was about. For a brief moment, he paused and stretched his mind tentatively toward the headquarters before going up to Annod's chamber. He was surprised to feel rays of warmth emanating from the man's mind. He had expected the man to be angry at his actions during the last three days.

The men in the mine had said nothing to him since the day before. Every time he had passed them, their eyes had fallen away from his, not daring to look directly at his. It wasn't anger. There was a certain respect for him, but they made him feel different, like the foreigner he was.

The servant was now tapping his foot impatiently on the stone steps, his tall figure casting a blinding shadow across Nadan's sight. Nadan noticed a hush had fallen over the men behind him. He knew they were interested in what was going to happen.

"Sir," the servant said, slight impatience tinging his voice. "My master is waiting." Following the servant, Nadan moved quickly up the steps and went through the heavy iron door that connected the headquarters to the mineshaft. The door was almost falling off its hinges and creaked loudly as he shut it behind him.

Annod was sitting in his chair, feet up on the table, a half-drunk glass of clinus sitting atop pages scattered across his desk. He leapt up immediately. Nadan noticed he was wearing a long formal red gown that seemed slightly out of place in the dank, cluttered headquarter room.

"Do come in, Nadan, and have a seat," he said, pointing to the chair opposite the table.

Annod had a strangely eager expression on his face. Nadan found it slightly unnerving, the man's veiled countenance, thinly belying hidden motivations. Nadan almost shuddered visibly, as Annod sat down again and ruffled some papers on the table with his fingers.

"That little scene you made in the mine . . ." Annod began. He halted mid-sentence.

"It was meant to create better relations, not worse, in the mine," Nadan interrupted.

"Well, yes, that's what I meant to talk to you about," said Annod.

Nadan was surprised again that he didn't sense more anger in the man's presence.

Annod rubbed his fingers across his chin, almost a smear, and leaned back in his chair. He gazed for a moment out the small dirt-spattered window that cast a faint glow of pale light into the room before speaking.

"Well, let me see. How shall I put it?" he said. "As you may already know, this mine is a subsidiary of a much larger mining company, known as the Quenna, which owns and oversees all the other mines in Valyna. There's a man by the name of Surya who's in charge of the whole mining operation. An important and powerful man. He pays very close attention to what's going on in the mines. He often gets reports from miners and other folks on both minor and major details of the operation."

"If I have upset him by my actions, I apologize," said Nadan. "That was not my intention."

Annod smiled, and his eyes shone for a moment. His fingers played across the papers on the table in front of him and then ruffled them again.

"No, actually quite the opposite," he said. "Surya was very interested and moved when he heard the story about you from another miner. He wants you to come meet with him tonight in the Quenna headquarters."

"I don't see why he would want to honor me in that way. I don't see it as such a significant thing that I did."

"It would look good if you went to meet him," said Annod, his eyes glinting politely.

Relying on his psychic powers, Nadan could detect that a layer of obsequiousness, as well as a touch of avarice, was flitting underneath the man's warm facial expression. For a moment, he believed he glimpsed the man's true intentions: Annod hoped to strengthen his partnership with Quenna and perhaps benefit financially from the exchange. Annod's mind was rife with a maze of details Nadan could still not discern or interpret. Still, he thought to himself, there was no harm in meeting this Surya . . .

"I will meet him," said Nadan, slowly. "I don't see any reason why I shouldn't."

"Excellent, boy," said Annod, getting up from his chair. He came over and patted Nadan lightly on the back, a friendlier touch than in the past. "Be sure to tell me tomorrow everything that happens."

Before saying goodbye, Annod gave him an electronic signaling device that told him where to turn on his way to the Quenna headquarters. Soon, Nadan was plodding out into the streets toward his destination. Snow was already beginning to fall in large flakes of crystalline white overhead. People stepping outside their kaaraadruun huts stared upward in wonder at the sight. Remembering it rarely snowed in this warm climate, Nadan smiled sentimentally. The scene, though oddly out of place in this sun-drenched city, was reminiscent of cold winters and snow festivals in Simkada. For a moment, it made him long for his homeland, but the feeling was quickly consumed by questions about what lay ahead of him. Was Surya Mandian? Is that why he was so "moved," as Annod said, by the incident in the mine? Or was this man simply more philanthropic, more socially progressive, than the average entrepreneur in Valyna?

After only a few minutes, Nadan felt pulsating vibrations on his hip, as the mapping device warned him he was nearing his destination. He was in the most affluent section of Valyna. Conical-shaped kaaraadruun huts, with elaborate gardens and trees and walkways, shot up through the darkening snow-fall around him. He turned and looked, seeing the Quenna Corporation sign looming above an arch over his head. Beyond it was a high-tiered kaaraadruun hut, with layers upon layers of mud-caked tiers stacked on top of each other like a giant staircase. Nadan noticed the numerous oval windows, which emanated a pale, greenish light from within, many of them so costly that they were emblematic of the highest aristocracy in Valyna. The place, however, seemed cold, dark, and brooding in the darkness of the street, barely illuminated by only a few scattered street globes. Nadan imagined it probably looked more inviting in the daytime.

He walked through the gate and followed the walkway to the door. The servant at the door opened the massive wooden door as soon as he touched the electronic bell device.

The hall he was led into was more lavish than anything he had ever seen in Simkada. Fountains sprayed high into the air, dancing over smooth mar-ble floors and colorful indoor gardens. High, arching ceilings bore more resemblance to a temple or court-yard than a place of commerce. People, clothed in gilded and silver robes, flitted through the space in the mellow glow.

"This way," the servant said, extending his palm toward a staircase to the side of the hall. Still staring at the fountains and impressive courtyard, Nadan followed the servant. The man was an elderly Val-ynan with a white beard and gentle, statesman-like eyes. Nadan could tell that he was quieter than oth-ers of his ethnicity.

As they walked slowly up the spiraling staircase, Nadan asked: "Does the Quenna ship acron to Simkada?"

"Yes, the Quenna is the only supplier of acron to the other cities," he said, dryly. "Without the corporation, your city, as well as Kira Mandi, would come to a halt."

Although he knew that all acron came from Valyna, Nadan had never heard that acron came into Simkada through a sole corporation. "I do not understand," said Nadan. "How did Quenna continue to supply Mandi with acron, even during the recent war? Wouldn't Valynan politicians have forced the Quenna to shut off all supplies to the city during the war?"

"It was tried but was never successful," said the man, dully. Nadan could tell from his voice he was uninterested in the matter, as if he had talked about it already too many times.

"The Quenna and its survival," the man added, after a moment's reflection, "was deemed more important than the war effort, which was only supported by a minority of Valynans."

Nadan couldn't help but wonder at the contradiction. He was unable to ask further, however, because the servant was now leading him up the long staircase more quickly. In a short time, the staircase ended, and Nadan found himself in another vast hallway. Pafnegu trees and other strange plants he had never seen before were spiraling up toward a high domed ceiling.

Tables and sitting mats had been scattered about below the vegetation. Parts of the polished marble floor were scattered with different colored rugs with red, green, and opal designs. But what caught

Nadan's attention immediately was the vast conical lumin-globe that thrust up into the direct center of the hallway. It cast a somber amber glow across the hallway, deepening the shadows in the hallway's corners and edges. In front of the lumin-globe was a tall man dressed in a golden robe that fell to the bottom of his feet. He was completely bald, and his head glinted with the amber light from the globe.

The man kept staring intently into the conical globe. As he drew closer, Nadan could soon see his face clearly in the light. His eyes were deep and introspective, ranging over bristling black ledges for eyebrows. Two birdlike azure eyes flitted back and forth over his hook-shaped nose. He almost looked like a bird of prey. Nadan could sense heavy matters were on his mind; the tiny wrinkles on his skin were taut, almost as if drained of all life and joy. With his wide forehead, Nadan would have almost said he looked Simkadan, except for the fact that the man had pale, marble-textured skin, a clear indication he was Valynan.

The man waved his hand at the servant. "Poyapa," he said quickly. Nadan knew the term meant "Leave us" in Valynan. Surya wrapped his arms around his back, clasping them together. The servant melted into the shadows.

The man smiled and for the first time in the city, Nadan felt more at ease with the natives than he had ever been. Surya's eyes fixed on him keenly for a second, and he felt the man's clear telepathic communication in his mind.

Your actions in the mine. What were you doing? the man telepathed.

He had not immediately sensed this man was an ajnir. Nadan's actions were poised, but his mind seemed less aware, in some way. He contemplated for a moment whether his expectations had deluded his perception into believing such a wealthy Valynan could not be an ajnir.

"You must be part of the Wheel of Thought, then," said Nadan.

"Yes, I work as precept in the Wheel," said the man. "I awoke as a child, but it wasn't until recently that they gave me that position."

They moved across the spacious hall together, side-by-side. As they went, Nadan cautioned himself: *This man could know—or be friends with—Sakr Ka.* He probed the man's thoughts for a moment but found he could discover nothing about the man's psychology.

The doorway at the end of the hallway opened into a lavish, cozy room. Large billowing cushions were spread out across the floor, and, as was the custom in Valyna, they both sat down opposite each other. Surya uncorked a clear bottle of purple liquid that rested on a golden platter at his feet.

"Clinus?" he asked.

"Thank you," said Nadan, taking the emerald-colored glass from the man.

Since he had become an ajnir, someone, he forgot who, had cautioned him to stay away from the inebriating drink. To what end, he was uncertain. But he believed that the drink dulled the refining process of his ajnir sensibilities. He liked drinking it, but he tended to minimize it, since his appaillama, his awakening as ajnir.

"Do all ajnir in Valyna drink clinus?" he asked.

"No, not usually," he said. "But I am a man of commerce, so I must partake of these things, you know, to adapt myself to the ways of the world in which I thrive. Isn't that how your teacher taught you?"

"I've heard that, but I've suddenly forgot who my teacher is for some reason."

Surya rubbed his chin for a moment, as he placed the stopper back into the glass bottle. But he seemed to suddenly grow uneasy. "The catacomb below here sometimes makes the memory sleep, so they say," the man said. "It was Manalk, wasn't it?"

"Yes, that was it," said Nadan, feeling embarrassed and not knowing what to say.

Surya then quickly changed subjects. To Nadan, he seemed as if he almost didn't want to insult his guest. "Tell me, Nadan, you have been working the mines, right?"

"Yes."

Nadan almost thought he caught a glimpse of amusement in Surya's face. "Well, we at the Wheel of Thought have always helped each other out. It is a code among us brothers and sisters of the Higher Order." Something in the way Surya said "higher order" painted pictures in Nadan's mind: ajnir as wisdom leaders from the ancient past, guiding and directing the city.

"You must understand," said Surya. "We ajnir are special, in one sense. We have powers that others don't. We read others' minds. We wield powers that others don't. Isn't it right that we should be leaders in society?" It was the first time that the thought had occurred to Nadan, but it seemed to make perfect sense.

"So what are you saying?" asked Nadan.

"Well, I was going to ask you if you might take a position with me at the Quenna," said Surya. "I have the perfect role for you, I think. You could be my second magistrate. It pays as well as your job in the mine, and I think you will find the work more to your liking and talents."

Nadan paused and thought for a moment. He reached his mind into the Watching, seeking its response. But, after a few moments, he stopped probing his own mind. He felt honored that Surya, this great powerful man in Valyna, had chosen him. Second magistrate. The position sounded important.

Surya was eyeing him carefully. Nadan sensed him reaching out deeply into his thoughts, threading his mind's fears and hesitations with his psychic ability."I will accept your offer," said Nadan.

Surya was about to say more, but then he paused. A bright orb was moving across the room. It swerved in the air, before coming up close to Surya's head. The man leaned forward, angled his eyes to his forehead position, and closed his eyes.

After a few moments, the orb moved slowly across the room again and vanished into the clay wall.

"What was that?" said Nadan.

"Oh, that's a telepath orb, a Wheel of Thought sphere," said Surya, casually. "Have you never seen one?" Nadan shook his head. "We ajnir use them when we may be having difficulty reaching our thoughts out to each other or finding another ajnir," Surya explained. "Walls and metals are a barrier sometime."

Nadan suddenly felt like he had been missing much, living in Simkada and never having been exposed to the Wheel of Thought. A wave of awe for Surya suddenly rippled through his consciousness. He felt weak and less capable than this great man who wielded both worldly and metaphysical powers with such ease and comfort.

"The orb just told me that I'm needed in the catacomb below," Surya said. "Would you like to accompany me as I walk down there?"

Nadan hesitated again. Would Sakr Ka be there? Yet this powerful ajnir had not tried to kill him. In case of danger, Nadan could recite the concealing meta and avoid notice. Yet his heart burned to see the ancient order's headquarters for some reason.

"Yes, I will come with you," said Nadan, at length.

Surya turned and moved to the wall. He pressed his finger on a small yellow button on the side of the wall, which had been hidden behind some cushions. The clay kaaraadruun wall suddenly parted in the middle and split with an almost imperceptible creaking sound.

"You often think deeply before you do anything," Surya observed. "That is good. I like that." He walked into the passage before him, and Nadan followed, warily, down a long dark stairway. His sandals clicked and echoed along the stone tunnel, but Surya padded almost silently, on his soft slipper-like shoes. Eventually, the staircase funneled into a narrow corridor with electric lumin-globes humming in the air overhead. The walls were pallid and white. Nadan noticed that some panels on the wall bore a symbol used by the Wheel of Thought: a perfect red circle enclosing a golden figure eight.

"This is the secret passage into the Ajnir Order of Quenna," Surya said. "The entire Ajnir Order is below ground in a catacomb. There are many such passages around the city which feed into the Wheel of Thought headquarters."

"Does anyone who isn't an ajnir ever break into the Wheel of Thought?" said Nadan.

"It happens rarely," said Surya. "But we've taken many precautions to make sure that there are no breaches. All the Quenna workers are ajnir, and they help to keep the order protected, with special attention to the main entrance. We also leave few traces of our presence in the catacomb itself. There is no writing, except for the ajnir symbol, on the walls in the catacomb. We leave no books or scrolls written about the ajnir in the open in the catacomb or its many chambers to ward against intruders learning of our presence."

"Are there no writings at all about the ajnir kept in the Order?" asked Nadan.

"Yes, there are very many," said Surya. "But they are kept in another secret vault even farther below ground. There is a vast crypt with all our ancient writings there. No intruder has ever accessed it in the millennia since the Order was formed."

Nadan had intentionally asked the question for another purpose. Toruna had spoken of the arthanti, the gem that can access the Dark Region of the Mazag dimension. His mind was churning with possibilities. Maybe he could access the gem and somehow discover Manalk's whereabouts. But he didn't dwell on the thought long. He didn't want Surya to discover his intentions through any psychic techniques.

As they moved along the corridor, they came to different doors, leading into separated side chambers. Nadan looked into one of them, a large room with a high ceiling and white walls. Small children, dressed in silver and blue robes, were scattered throughout the room, painting with long, arm-length brushes on what looked like large canvases spread out at their feet.

"That is the artists' chamber," said Surya. "We have many chambers here, where ajnir can learn to express their talents. We have rooms for music, athletics, combative fight . . ." Surya was counting them on his fingers, trying to remember. "And a knowledge or metaphysics room," he said. "But that is below ground in the crypt."

"How are these different from what they learn in schools in Valyna?" asked Nadan.

"Well, we understand that ajnir often are unable to show their true natures in public, so we have allowed them these educational centers to provide a channel for their natural propensities," said Surya. "Our approach allows ajnir, especially young ones, to understand and learn with others like themselves."

Nadan stared at the children in the room. For a moment, he wondered what he would have been like if he had been discovered as a young child in Valyna. Would he have learned the ajnir ways much better? Would his ability to reach into the Watching be more advanced?

"I must go talk with someone here privately, but you may walk around the rooms, as you like," said Surya. "I may be an hour or so. You may gain access to the lower crypt, if you like, and read there."

He turned to leave, but Nadan suddenly spoke. "Do you ever think the Order will be revealed to the public?" he asked. It had been something he had often wondered. He had asked Manalk once, but the ajnir had simply smiled in his familiar, enigmatic way and said nothing.

Surya gave him a strange but curious glance. Nadan almost thought he detected distrust in the man's probing hazel eyes, now black, murky pools in the dim light. "It has been talked about much before in the past," he said. "But most do not think it would be a good thing. If the public masses were to know about the Hidden Realms and the subtle powers, they would certainly misuse them . . ."

He paused in the middle of his response. Nadan tried to probe his thoughts again but felt himself pushing against a mass of dark, swirling energy that repelled his mind. He sensed Surya was about to state his own opinion on the subject but had suddenly stopped.

Surya smiled. "Well, I must be going," he said. "But perhaps we can talk about this later."

He turned and strode down the hall, his robe swishing softly. The amber lumin-globe at his feet swayed delicately in the air as he brushed past it; fractured rays of lights skittered across the ceiling.

Nadan turned and looked into the room with the children painting. He walked slowly inside. He had never been around so many ajnir before, and he had never met one who was a child. He wasn't quite sure what to expect. He sensed a strange electricity moving through the room, the same he had felt when he had touched the arthanti. For a moment, he forgot his surroundings and lost himself in the scintillating electrical current.

The children in the room painted silently and intently, ignoring him. In the far corner of the room, there was a girl who seemed a little older than the rest. She was tall for her age with large dimples and smooth, silky skin. Her small eyes were a deep shade of amber mixed with blue. She was stooping forward over the canvas at her feet, staring intently at him. Her gaze was almost unnerving to Nadan in its complete awareness. She seemed to be seeing right through him, to the bubbles of thought at the surface of his mind and even deeper into the thoughts that lay beneath his conscious mind.

"Are you a new teacher?" she asked.

"I might be," he said, coming toward her.

The girl suddenly telepathed into his mind, clearly and distinctly: *I have seen you before.*

Where? asked Nadan.

In a dream.

The girl went over to the corner of the room. For the first time, Nadan noticed that there were shelves embedded in the wall so that they blended in with the wall surface. The girl pulled the shelf out and ruffled through the papers inside. After a moment, she pulled out a canvas sheet smaller than the one she had been working on and handed it to him. Nadan took out his telescoping glasses from his robe and fitted them on his nose. The background of the painting was a drab-colored gray, tinged with shadows of black. There was a desk in the right corner with a lumin-globe on it, casting yellow rays onto a person sprawled out on the floor. The boy's upturned face was looking at the ceiling into an amber orb. It was his face.

The thin canvas fell from Nadan's hand and onto the floor. "How many times have you watched me?" he asked, after a moment. "My remote vision isn't all that good. I see yours is much better."

The girl picked up the canvas and carefully folded it. "It was a month ago," she said. "I forget when. Visions here and there. The look on your face interested me. I became aware of you after you saw that uriel."

"Have you seen one of those creatures yourself?"

"I've never seen them. But others of us have."

"Who saw them?"

The girl's eyes fell. Nadan knew there was much she wasn't saying. He knew the Wheel of Thought believed the uriel were illusions. It was obvious the girl was scared to speak of them in the headquarters. He recited the concealing meta to ward off his thoughts and conversation from other ajnir in the vicinity.

At that moment, a bell clanged in the air, echoing along the hall. The children, who had been silent, suddenly started rustling, putting away their canvases in shelves along the vast white wall.

"It's fine," said Nadan. "You can tell me."

"It's time to go," said the girl. She looked suddenly nervous.

"What is your name?"

"Naria."

"I'm Nadan." He smiled warmly. The lines of her face remained tense. Nadan sensed the talk of the uriel had upset her. Naria picked up the canvas at her feet and stowed it in the wall, locking it with a silver key. "I hope to see you again," said Nadan. Naria smiled again quickly but said nothing. Then she walked toward the corridor where Nadan had entered.

Nadan stayed where he was. Stretching his mind out for a moment, he sensed that there were other ajnir around, who were constantly monitoring the area with their minds. Naria had probably been concerned about their presence. He sensed that they hadn't been. But some might also have the same repelling ability as Surya, he thought. At that moment, he felt a strange meta in his mind, a forgetting, dispelling spell that sounded like the word klana, resounding in his mind, and he remembered that his master was Manalk, and that he was missing, and the day he was imprisoned in the cave with a drug inside him by Valynan soldiers. And the girl Naria was speaking to him in his mind, saying: *They made you forget. The Wheel people. Your master is in Mazag. It's mirroring. This is something he did to someone once, a long time ago.*

The Wheel did that? he replied, but at that moment, he had to mask his thoughts, because a woman in a silver robe weaved through the crowd of children toward him. "Hakij," she said in Valynan. Her voice was quiet but had an attractive self-assurance that quieted the children down immediately. Nadan knew the phrase meant "Quiet down" in Valynan, but he couldn't understand the rest of what the woman said to the children. Nadan's mind was distracted with all that had just happened, as the children departed down the corridor, their voices echoing off the stone walls.

"Simrulde," she said, holding out her thin fingers to him. "Surya told me to guide you around the headquarters, as you wait." Like Naria he felt this woman had the same ability to peer through his mind, as if exploring every crevice of his inner being. He only half heard the question, but muttered back politely, "I'd like that."

The woman stepped closer to him. "Is something wrong?" she asked. Nadan quickly concealed his thoughts with a meta.

"No, just overwhelmed."

The children's voices dimmed further in the chamber, as they moved into the corridors. Nadan regained his composure, wondered if she might be probing the Watching about what was going on in his mind.

They walked out of the hall and moved along the corridor, side by side. Simrulde pointed out the different chambers as they went along. Unlike in the children's area, thin, almost transparent curtains draped across the doorways of the other chambers.

"Some of our children already have psychic abilities when they come," explained Simrulde. "So it is important that they not learn any spells or metaphysical powers which they might use in a reckless way. These curtains are made from a special fiber that repels telepathing into the rooms, so others can practice their skills."

Nadan stretched his mind out for a second and felt his thoughts encounter a black shadow. It felt similar to the strange, repelling mass that enshrouded the mind of Surya. "I would like to visit the crypt below," said Nadan. "Would that be possible, or is it off-limits to outsiders?"

"It is heavily protected," said Simrulde. "You will need clearance to enter the place."

But Surya has given you clearance . . . she mused telepathically.

She lifted up her arm and mumbled words into a region near her wrist. Nadan realized that she had an intercom installed inside the skin under her wrist. He had read about it in Simkada but never seen it himself. It was said the operation was costly.

"Why do you want to enter the sanctum?" asked Simrulde. "The guards would like to know."

"I have never read any books written by the ancient ajnir, except for one," said Nadan. "I'm particularly interested in the subject of the uriel."

Simrulde turned her head sharply to look at him. Her blue sapphire-like eyes were well controlled, always pleasant. Nadan, however, could tell that she was startled, the way her eyelids seemed to wince subtly as she looked at him. She paused for a minute, as if carefully thinking over what to say next. Then, she spoke into her wrist again in Valynan.

"They will let you in," she said, finally.

She led him down another long corridor, with steps that traversed downward at angles into another corridor. The walls were painted bright gold, but the corridor was narrower, so they couldn't walk side by side. Simrulde led Nadan down the corridor, her soothing voice echoing along the metal tunnel. "You speak of the uriel, as if you know of them well," she said, looking back toward him. "That at least is what I sense in you."

"I encountered one back in Simkada," said Nadan. "You could say I'm interested in the subject."

Again, Nadan had the same sense that Simrulde was alarmed, almost wincing inside. He felt the issue was something nearer to her heart, as if the subject reminded her of some unspeakable tragedy still too near and painful. He opened his mouth to ask her more, but then the corridor ended. Simrulde stopped walking and pressed her finger against the wall. The golden panels of the corridor folded inward, and two Valynan warriors stepped out of the space, their face masks tilted up along their heads.

"You are only permitted 15 gryas in the crypt," said Simrulde. "Everyone must leave the Wheel of Thought by nightfall. It is the law."

"Why are there no people allowed in at night?" said Nadan.

"Too much traffic during the night would draw attention," said one of the warriors. His mouth reverberated through a voice modulator at his throat. "Only the princeps of the Wheel of Thought are allowed in at night."

The warrior moved back into the secret passage, along with the other warrior. Nadan walked past Simrulde and into the shaft. It was completely dark, but a dull golden light shone through the screen of metal below their feet. Simrulde bowed low in Eroni fashion without a word, and her form melted in the shadows. Nadan stood with his back against the shaft, as the golden doors folded inward again, leaving them in darkness.

He heard the Valynan warrior next to him tapping his metallic gloves along the wall. He tried to read the man's mind, but it was repelled.

"What are you doing?" said Nadan.

"It is a code to give us access to the crypt," said the man, after a moment. His voice modulator was now turned off, and he spoke in a deep, gravelly Valynan accent.

An engine sputtered and began whirring quietly. Suddenly, the shaft shivered and moved downward swiftly. Nadan felt his stomach rising dizzily into his chest, but it only lasted a few seconds. When the shaft came to a rest, the warrior again tapped his metallic gloves on the wall, and the doors folded inward again, almost whisking their faces as it opened.

The Valynan warriors moved out into the space beyond, Nadan behind them. He found himself in a small antechamber. Lumin-globes, suspended from the low ceilings, chimed and wavered in a draft flowing through the place, casting a mix of red and gold light around the chambers. Low shelves of scrolls and books diverged in different angles from the ante-chamber itself. This was not like the grand under-ground catacombs Nadan was used to in Simkada, but he didn't expect it to be either. This was Valyna, a city not known for its lore and learning. But at the same time, he felt his heart and mind even more thrilled than when he had first entered the ancient crypts of Simkada years ago as a child. These were all scrolls, containing profound secrets of an ancient society few in history had ever accessed.

A short old woman, wearing clear telescoping glasses, walked toward him silently from one of the darkened aisles. A smoky white braid of hair fell across the front of her dark mantle that fell to her ankles. She was holding a scroll and metallic device in both hands.

Her quiet, slow movements intimated a familiar rhythm. "You are Simkadan," he said, as she drew closer.

"I grew up there," she said, as if recalling a bad memory. Her voice carried a clear Simkadan accent that stirred Nadan's memories of his homeland. "I used to work in the catacombs of Simkada many years ago," she said. "But when I heard about the Wheel of Thought, I knew I had to come see it for myself. There was so much to learn here that I couldn't learn from things I read in Simkada."

"Not many Simkadans have ever done that. Do you feel alienated?"

"To an extent, sometimes. But I have found myself more at home in Valyna for some reason."

She paused for a second, then extended her wrinkled palm: "I am Kalaso, by the way."

"Nadan," he returned, glancing stiffly around the crypt. She took his palm in hers and grasped it warmly for a second. But her face quickly became sad and anxious.

"Since the truce with Simkada was shattered, the soldiers here have been watching me carefully, however, and I no longer feel so at peace here," she said, after a moment, as if wondering whether she should speak of the matter. "They know I come from Simkada, and they wonder whether I will talk to my family in Simkada. I have never been a spy, nor ever will be. The few Simkadans here are not looked upon well enough as before, but not nearly as bad as the Mandians."

"What have you heard of the war?"

"There was a campaign to the north by our army here a few days ago. Simkadans gained some of our territory but not much. Rak Pow, our general of arms, gave us few clues about the new war. But our city is against it for the most part. They tell me that you want to learn more about the uriel."

He nodded thoughtfully.

"It is a strange subject," said Kalaso. "Not many have written about it; only a few have in the last 20 years or so."

Kalaso lifted up her hand and held out the electronic device in her palm, as if offering it to Nadan. Then she reached out and, with her bony, wrinkled index finger, began writing words on the device with what looked like a small piece of chalk attached to the end of her fingernail. She turned and waved for Nadan to follow. The Valynan warriors returned to the shaft where he had entered, their boots clicking on the stone floor. Nadan watched the silver doors fold back together without a sound. Then he followed Kalaso along the aisles.

Chapter 8

The Mazag

Kalaso's dark robe fluttered in the air, mixing with the dull, opaque shadows lining the aisles. There were only a few lumin-globes scattered about, suspended by long wires. Their brightness created sharp contrasts between the light and shadows along the narrow aisle.

Nadan glanced at the backs of the scrolls as he walked. The titles he could see, inscribed in golden letters on the backs of the faded parchment, were written in the strange symbols of the ajnir language he had only begun to learn from Manalk. He managed to decipher one when Kalaso stopped for a moment to brush a cobweb off a lumin-globe. It said: *The History and Development of Traloming.*

Nadan stretched his hand out and rubbed his fingers across the gold letters. He had no idea what traloming was.

"It means telepathing," said Kalaso, turning to gaze at him quizzically.

She had obviously read his mind. Nadan pulled his finger from the scroll, almost as if he had been touching something he wasn't supposed to. He had forgotten that he was with someone who had the same abilities he had.

Kalaso seemed unconcerned. She turned and waved her hand forward casually, urging him along the aisle. They walked for a few seconds, and then Kalaso stopped and stood up on her toes. Nadan, who was much taller, walked over, and she pointed toward a scroll on the top of one shelf. He reached up, grabbed the large scroll between his fingers, and stepped down again.

"These are the most widely read writings on the legendary uriel," said Kalaso.

She handed him a small metal disc of paper, which felt heavier than it looked, and said: "I will be in the front of the crypt."

Kalaso and her dark robe melted into the deep shadows of the crypt. Nadan sat down at a nearby table and opened the scroll carefully, letting the end drape over the table and onto the soft red carpet at his feet. It was written in the common tongue but in Valyna's dashing script, small, circular shapes, letters and symbols he had been learning over the past few months. It made for slow reading, but he was soon able to discover that it was dated in the year 45037 PFE, some 50 years ago, and had been written by an ajnir by the name of Dasra.

Over the next hour, he pored ravenously over the parchment. Dasra, a scientist from the Wheel of Thought, had compiled numerous accounts, documenting his interviews with people across Urshan Dai who had reported experiences with the uriel. He had specifically been charged to advise the Order about the nature of the phenomenon, which at the time was becoming unusually common. The sightings had been cross-cultural, occurring within all the three major cities. That had eventually awoken the Wheel of Thought's interest, and a formal investigation had ensued.

The scroll documented numerous cases of strange, apparition-like creatures that mirrored Nadan's own experiences. To his disappointment, Dasra didn't record any of the strange messages that people reported from the creatures. He was even more disappointed when the writer ended his account by siding with leading scientists of the day in attributing the phenomenon to the effect of geomagnetic shifts in the planet's core.

"The apparent vacillating light effect, so common in many cases, is the result of an unusual psychological inducement relating to geomagnetic aberrations that have been shown to exert hallucinatory pressures on the psyche. That this has happened only in the last 100 years should not surprise us, given the geological changes that our planet has witnessed in the last century. The gibberish phrases that those interviewed report is only further proof that these encounters are not contacts with intelligible beings but the result of random, psychological synapses."

Nadan wrapped the scroll up tightly again and walked slowly back to the front of the crypt. Kalaso was sitting at a desk, hunched over a parchment, the silver metal rims of her telescoping glasses nearly touching the pages in front of her. Her silver hair shone like dull armor under a lumin-globe over her head.

Nadan put the scroll down in front of her on the desk.

"Are there any writings that hold the opposite view to this one?" he asked.

Kalasa pulled off her telescoping glasses with her long fingers and rested them on the page in front of her. "There were some early on, but they gained little favor in the Order, after this scroll was published," she said, distractedly. "That writing you just read came to be the authoritative text on the issue. This crypt doesn't contain any of the other writers with opposing views, I believe. Few are now in print."

"I would like to look at some if possible. Are there any that you know of that are available in this city?"

"I could intercom the other crypts in the city and find out. It may take some time. You may browse the crypt in the meantime, if you like."

As Kalaso talked on an intercom, Nadan moved about the aisles again, browsing the titles idly and stopping every now and then to open a scroll. Most of the scrolls he found were fairly uninteresting, dealing with the regulations and legal underpinnings of the Quenna and the Wheel of Thought. But he did come across a few interesting works, including a work of ajnir poetry, which he read eagerly over the next hour. By the time he had finished it, Kalaso had still not contacted all the other crypts in the city, so he walked again around the aisles looking at the pictures of ajnir leaders lining the outer wall.

As he was halfway around the crypt, in the direct middle of the rectangular chamber, he stopped to look at a large ajnir symbol mounted on a pedestal: a great golden wheel of metal that was hemmed on each side by tall plants and two paintings of venerable seers. Even as he stopped, he felt a strange purring in his ear, as if a moth made of air was fluttering inside his eardrum. He looked over and he saw a golden orb, dancing as if in an imaginary wind. He knew immediately it was a telepath orb, much like he had witnessed a short time ago in the Quenna headquarters with Surya.

The orb nuzzled into his ear again.

I can help you find your teacher.

Nadan's heart almost stopped. His hands trembled.

Who are you? he telepathed back.

A friend.

But what is your name?

My name is irrelevant. I can help you find the Mazag arthanti.

Manalk had once mentioned the gem that granted access to the Mazag, the dark dimension, and that it was off limits to most in the order.

How did you know Manalk was in Mazag? he asked.

The orb shook and shivered.

He was put there by the Wheel. They have meta devices that do that.

Follow me, it said finally, after a pause.

The light circled in the air and then bobbed its way further down the aisles. Nadan wondered at its motion. It seemed to move effortlessly, like Manalk himself, dancing and playing through its existence like an ecstatic insect. He sensed this was a different kind of orb from the one he had seen before. It had a friendly and uninhibited radiance, almost like a child's mind.

When they reached the end of the aisle, Nadan noticed that a door-opening keypad with symbols and letters was linked to the wall. He had walked by it before, noting that it seemed odd that there was no door.

The orb moved across the strange ajnir letters on the surface of the keypad.

Follow my movements and push the letters.

As the orb moved across four different symbols—a figure-eight symbol, a gorlon bird, a ram, and a lizard—Nadan pushed them with his finger slowly. He had to press them down hard before they snapped back into an indentation in the wall. Finally, when he had pressed them all, the walls folded inward, leading into a cavernous blackness. He went forward and felt the walls for a lumin-switch. After minutes of groping, he found one, and the light from above illuminated a gray stone-walled room with featureless walls and a narrow glass shelf, lined with scrolls and small books with red and black bindings. The air in the chamber felt colder than that in the main crypt. The walls folded in again by themselves, and he was alone inside the room.

Where is the arthanti? he asked the orb.

The orb hovered a moment and then disappeared into the wall without responding. Nadan sighed and walked over to the shelves. There were only about a dozen books on the shelf; he took them out each in turn, examining each of their bindings. He opened them but found nothing.

Finally, he pulled a tiny book off the shelf, one that was hidden behind two large, impressively sized scrolls. Its binding was made of tough, hardened leather, and it bore no name, except a tiny phrase at the bottom in golden letters, which said, in the ajnir tongue, "Paintings of an ancient world." He knew instantly something was different about the book. The familiar energy of an arthanti seethed in his palm, oscillating and vibrating up through his arm. It was a slightly different sort of energy than

Manalk's arthanti: it felt colder, more seductive. He opened the book and saw a gleaming black gem embedded within its pages. Then he shut it, put the book down for a second, and detached himself from the feeling.

At that moment, the orb reemerged from the wall and moved close to his head. Nadan felt its cozy, humming sound in his ear again.

Be cautious, it said, mentally.

I will, he thought.

He hesitated.

Do you know where my teacher might be inside that world? he asked.

I do not.

The orb dissolved in the wall again. Nadan sensed it would not come back to help him this time. He sighed again and opened the book once more, looking at the facets of the onyx gem scintillating in the faint light of the crypt. The object was a dangerous tool, he knew, but he had learned much from his training with Manalk. He sensed he could now better handle and control the abrupt inflow of energy that the ancient gems created in the body. At the same time, he was worried. Manalk had never said anything about the arthanti leading to the dark universe. Could this gem be more dangerous than the ones that lead to the Dinjin? He knew his time would be limited in the Dark Regions of Mazag: an ajnir could keep his mind in such a universe only for a brief time before his thoughts rebelled and returned to his native reality. It was the law of the dimensional worlds, Manalk had told him. No one was designed to live in a universe he had not been born in. He would have to act swiftly if he wanted to speak to his master.

Nadan reached out hesitantly and placed his finger on a faceted side of the gem. The scenery around him changed instantly. He was standing on a dirt road, winding along a desolate landscape. A crimson sky shone out brightly beyond dark, jagged shapes of mountains that stretched like a broken row of teeth along the horizon. Noiseless lightning flashed in the distance, over the rim of dim mountains. After a few moments, a thunderclap resounded in the air, drowning the silence. He thought he heard voices of anguish revolving inside the sound, but they halted as soon as he focused his attention on them. A shadow moved in front of him and disappeared into the hill of red soil to his right.

"Who's there?" he called out loudly, in terror. His throat became clogged with a strange substance, like the dust of moth wings, and he coughed. He called again but he heard no response in the heavy air.

He looked around for a moment more, and then he found that the gem was lying in his palm. He turned it over again in his palm and placed his thumb across another symbol. A new scene flashed before his eyes. He was in a great hall, with flickering lamps and a high, arching ceiling. A long table, covered in glass tubes and small, whirring machines, stretched along the length of the chamber. He was reminded of the ancient castles he had seen depicted in books of ancient Urshan Dai, except none of them, at that point in history, had discovered machines yet. He eyed them more closely. One had a wheel spinning inside a glass tube, gyrating, with a green smoke thickening and billowing inside it. He walked over and looked at the papers at its base. The dialect was unintelligible: harsh, black strokes and lines splintering in different directions.

A shadowy figure moved along the other side of the table, an old man, it looked like. Two luminous, glimmering yellow eyes leered out at him from the darkness.

"What's your name?" asked Nadan, his voice rising and falling soundlessly in the air.

But the man quickly turned his face away and stared at the tubes steaming on the table in front of him. His heart sank for a moment. He realized this quest of his might be a fruitless effort. He would never find the ajnir this way. He moved to the back of the stone wall behind him and thought for a moment, watching the man move gracefully among the tubes and experiments. He was obviously a scientist, some sort of chemist. His hood was now thrown back on his shoulders, and Nadan could now see his face clearly. He was bald, with a sly grin trickling across a pallid face smudged with thick streaks of dirt or ink. His features were ugly; his eyes seemed to gleam maniacally in the faint light. His fingers danced among the tubes, like dragonfly wings. Nadan shuddered at the sight. He wanted to leave this place.

He had just opened his palm to look at the arthanti again when something strange happened. He suddenly had the sensation that he was on the other side of the room, staring at the scientist's back instead of his face. It felt as if his body was a light particle that had abruptly jumped from one side of the room to the other. Then, all of a sudden, he was back to where he had been standing before. But something was different. The scientist's sly, impish smile had faded from his crinkled features. He was no longer toying over his experiments. He was staring at him, startled, with his mouth gaping open.

"How did you get in here?" the man asked in a harsh, weathered voice.

Chapter 9

Reunion

Nadan retreated against the stone wall. It seemed as if the sounds in the room became sharper, more distinct. The machines on the table whirred and whined deeply, and a tube along the table bubbled sonorously.

The man came from around the table, brandishing what looked like a large cast-iron pole.

"I did not see the door open, yet you are here," the man said. "Are you from the ward?"

Nadan didn't know what to say. He was totally baffled that he was actually in Mazag, not an unseen observer in this world, as Toruna had told him.

The man came closer, eyeing him with a malevolent, suspicious expression that made Nadan shiver deeply inside.

"You are from the ward, aren't you?" he said, grimly. "You people are always coming to thieve my mixes. I will need to talk to Brakin about this. This cannot happen any longer."

He shook a gnarled finger at the bubbling, frothing tubes, taking a rough step closer. Nadan suddenly came to his senses. He realized he had to defend himself.

"I come from another world," he said.

The man laughed uproariously, his harsh, brusque voice grating and echoing in the hall, like an unoiled metal wheel.

"You ward folk tell every little lie imaginable," he said, finally. "This one tops them all. So where do you come from? What world might this be?"

"I come from a place called Simkada," said Nadan, not knowing what else to say. "It is in another universe. I came with the help of this gem."

Nadan held out the dark gem so the man could see it, but the man didn't wait any longer. He swung his iron pole around quickly, but Nadan, who was aware of his thoughts, ducked and ran. The man was too old to pursue and stopped to shout after him.

"And don't come back, you gargul," he yelled.

Nadan ran quickly to the doorway of the hall and opened it. A blast of cold wind struck his face as he ran out into the pitch-blackness beyond. He ran for a few minutes and then looked back. No one was pursuing him. He was in a lowland area with dark scrubs and scant trees hemming him in on each side of the road. Impenetrable clouds ranged over his head, like blackened, indolent sheep straying over a shadowy, transparent grassland. He kept walking down the small, faint road ahead of him.

Then, it dawned on him: if he could be seen in this world, he could certainly telepath with Manalk. Immediately, he stretched out with his thoughts, piercing the black shadow world around him. It was as if his thoughts were plunging through a dense, murky pond; his mental fibers felt like dense, cumbersome algae swaying and waving about inside it. He paused, concentrating deeply for almost a minute. Soon, his mind adjusted to the dark mass of energy blocking his mind. The atmosphere felt strange. It was as if his mind had plunged through the layers of murk and entered a vast, ambient horizon that was somehow above him and nowhere at the same time. His thoughts were now piercing through the otherworldly atmosphere with ease, rapidly, with no resistance. And to his surprise, for some unexplainable reason, he felt his telepathic range could extend further in this place. He sat down on the ground, crossing his legs on the dirt road. His thoughts went out further, until suddenly he felt a glimmer of response at some remote end of the world he was on. Or, perhaps, was it another planet? It didn't matter. He felt Manalk's mind somewhere in the dark, filthy, nebulous clouds of this world.

Master, master, he telepathed. He was suddenly afraid he would leave this world soon.

You shouldn't have come here, came the response after a moment. *But I'm nevertheless glad to sense your inner voice again.*

An indescribable thrill went through his being. Hopes swept aside the darkness of his vision. He was back again, with his master. The aloof, yet near, presence of his master permeated his consciousness.

Oh master, you must come back.

I cannot come back yet. I may never come back.

But why? Why did you leave? You knew they would come for you.

Manalk did not respond for a long moment, almost a minute. Nadan listened to the gnawing loneliness of the landscape around him, sighing and heaving with anguish, like a deep, murky, forgetful ocean.

Sand does not become glass until it is heated by fire, Manalk responded finally. It was a distant and cool communication.

Nadan smiled for a brief moment at Manalk's enigmatic response, so familiar from his days in training. But his thoughts were moving quickly, too quickly. The connection between Manalk's mind and his broke for a moment, as if the wind had picked up their thoughts and dispersed them, like dust. After a minute of calming his mind, he regained the connection. He had lost some of what the ajnir was saying.

The time is coming for you . . . but he missed the rest. He concentrated again quickly, increasing the connection.

Toruna said you might be able to jump between universes, Nadan interjected, ignoring what he had missed. *You must be able to do that.*

It is possible.

Your place is not in this world, master, said Nadan, vehemently.

For right now, it is. You will understand someday.

Manalk's inner voice was like murmuring clouds.

Nadan was preparing to argue the point, when he felt his head suddenly swimming. Again, he felt like a light particle, shifting between different locations along the landscape. Then, the land before him glimmered once and disappeared, folding in on itself like ethereal tissues that roll up in the air and vanish. Manalk's mind dwindled in the atmosphere and was gone, and Nadan was lying on his back in the crypt, back in the Wheel of Thought headquarters.

He rolled over onto his side. The gem was on the floor next to him. He grabbed at it and placed his fingers again on the symbols. Nothing happened. He flung it on the ground, listening to it crack against the wall. It was as he had been told by Toruna. One can only access the arthanti every few days. Once the gem is used, the mind refuses to return to the alternate realities, the ajnir had said.

He lay still on the ground for a moment, composing himself. Then he breathed deeply twice and stood up. He picked up the small gem and placed it inside the same small book, then put the book on the shelf. Finally, he stepped to the walls and pushed on them gently. They folded in on themselves, smoothly and silently. He walked into the crypt again, the walls quietly snapping shut behind him.

He projected his mind out across the aisles for a moment. He had not been detected. Kalaso's mind was buzzing with thoughts about some man named Salata whom Nadan didn't know. He walked along the aisles and met her, close to the folding gates where he had entered with the Valynan warriors.

Kalaso took off her telescoping glasses and looked at him.

"No other crypts in the city that I have contacted have scrolls written on the subject you asked about," she said. "It is strange. Apparently, there was recent interest from many Mandians in those writings just two years ago. The crypts in possession of those writings have all sold them."

"Well, thanks for taking such efforts to find them," said Nadan. "But I think I should be getting back to Surya now."

Even as he spoke, the walls next to him rippled and collapsed inward. Out of the darkness beyond strode the tall, magisterial form of Surya.

"I thought I would find you down here," he said. "I know you Simkadans and books are inseparable." Surya's smile had the same forced composure that Nadan had noticed the first time he met him. He wondered: *Does he know that I accessed the arthanti?*

"You could have found me by using your telepathy," Nadan remarked.

"No," said Surya. "This room is protected on all sides with a mind-repellant alloy. It is an important safety precaution by which we can keep this place as secret as possible."

It made sense to Nadan now. Whoever had helped him discover the Mazag arthanti needed the telepath orb to communicate with him. Surya turned and smiled, gesturing to the door.

After thanking Kalaso again, Nadan followed Surya into the elevator and moved upward into the pitch blackness, the cage humming around them. The doors folded inward, and they walked along the corridors of the Wheel of Thought again while Surya continued their discussion where he had left off, cataloguing the ancient history of the ancient order. Nadan asked fewer questions this time, since he was preoccupied with his recent experience with the arthanti. The Mazag universe had left an indelible impression on his mind. He felt strangely downcast after the experience, and he sensed his mood wasn't necessarily related to the fact that he was unable to convince Manalk to return to this universe. He felt as if the dark matter that permeated that universe still clung to his consciousness, like a lifeless clump of moss. And yet at the same time, he felt his powers of telepathy were suddenly more acute, more alert, than they had ever been. Does the Mazag actually increase an ajnir's psychic abilities?

He pondered that question as Surya led him up back into his chamber and along the rows of potted plants and bubbling fountains inside the stately kaaraadruun hut where they had first met. Eventually, they came to the entrance to the building. Surya had talked so much during the walk that he had failed to realize Nadan was only half listening to him. Finally, at the entrance, he turned to look at Nadan.

"My friend, you are pale," he said. "You look weary. Has the mining job been too difficult today?"

"I am just overwhelmed with everything I've seen here," he said.

"Ah, well, the order has many profound secrets," said Surya. "Come by tomorrow, and we will discuss your new position."

"I will," said Nadan.

Surya turned quickly and disappeared into the entrance of the Quenna. With a half smile, Nadan departed out the path, leading into the mansion hut. The snow outside was still falling, and several inches had already accumulated on the ground outside. Children were frolicking on the edges of the street. Their voices echoed and reverberated on the huts in the pleasantly stifling air.

Chapter 10

Naria

Nadan walked slowly past the children on the street outside the Wheel of Thought headquarters. He felt slightly ill. His stomach gyrated angrily. His consciousness seemed to be swilling in the air, moving rapidly in and about the snowflakes, as if his thoughts had somehow fused with their erratic motions. He wondered if he was experiencing some strange aftereffect of the arthanti. A peculiar phrase kept resounding in his mind: *Time is the captive caterpillar.*

He walked more quickly down the street, retracing his steps back to his hut. After he had gone a few blocks, he felt out of breath and sat down on the stone steps under the lee of one of the shops. He had sat there for several minutes before he noticed that someone was standing across the street. The person was small framed and wore a crimson cloak that contrasted sharply with the somber granite wall behind.

Nadan wondered how the person had stood there for so long without his noticing. *It must be an ajnir with concealing capabilites*, he thought to himself.

The figure moved out from the shelter of the building and threw back a blue, gaping hood. It was Naria.

It had felt like days since he had seen her. The time spent in the Mazag had distorted his sense of time. Or was it just that that place was so different from this world, it made the day's mundane events seem like distant clouds?

Naria moved across the street toward him. As she drew closer and joined him under the lee of the shop, she said: "I knew I could meet you here."

Nadan traced the caverns of her awareness for a moment.

"You knew I was in the crypt, didn't you?" he said.

Naria's face turned the color of the ashen gray wall across the street for a moment. Then, she reached into a pocket in the side of her robe and drew out a long, thin veil for blocking telepathy.

"We need to put this over our heads," she said quickly. With a swift motion of her arm, Naria threw the veil over his head.

"We should move to the alley," said Nadan, taking the veil off quickly. "This will look too weird, standing here."

Stuffing the veil in his pocket, he led her into the narrow lane near the edge of the road. Some cats were poking their noses into the small, slit-like holes of gilak, urban rodents with long red tails, which had burrowed their way into the base of the kaaraadruun huts along the lane. The street was fairly dark, but a lumin-globe cast a single thin, somber ray of blue energy. Nadan led Naria around the pack of cats and stood under the lee of a small, rotund kaaraadruun hut further down the street. Together, backs against the wall of the restaurant, they huddled, their heads close together now. Nadan pulled out the veil and placed it over both their heads. Their breaths blew a whitish foggy mist at each other in alternating rhythms.

"I want to tell you . . ." her voice stopped again. A strange light had moved out of her pocket and was hovering in the air next to them.

"It was *your* telepath orb," Nadan cried out, sharply.

Naria smiled demurely but also slightly mischievously. She reached out and cupped the orb between her fingers. She muttered a few secret syllables in the ajnir language. When she opened her hands again, the orb had disappeared.

"Yes, it was me," she said, finally.

"How did you know the code on the panel?" asked Nadan.

"Oh, that was easy," she said. "A head ajnir was coming out of the crypt last month, and I read his mind. He was preoccupied and forgot to conceal himself. I hope you enjoyed talking to your teacher again."

"It was truly a great gift you gave me," said Nadan. "I don't know how I can ever repay you. But I fear that I will never see him again."

Nadan felt like his voice was falling into the small hole in the stone at the base of the street. Naria diverted her eyes for a second, looking downward. Finally, Nadan spoke again. "You came here to tell me something else, however," he said.

Naria's bluish, mystical eyes met his, then fell again to the street, despondently. "The uriel have come to this place many times," she said, finally.

"To the city?"

"No, to the Order. Many of us children have seen them and some adults too. But mostly, the children. It began several months ago."

"But haven't the uriel been coming for many years before this?"

"Oh yes," said Naria, "But not like this. It used to happen maybe once a year or so. The Order was able to deal with it quietly then. But now, many are having the experiences. The Order is troubled."

"And yet they forbid you to talk of it."

"They didn't at first. They allowed many to talk about their experiences. They would often tell us they were just dreams and hallucinations. But, now, too many are experiencing the visitations. They became overwhelmed by the reports, and eventually they ruled out any talk of them."

"What happens if someone talks about it?"

"Different things. Fadakoa, one of our friends, spoke about it, and they put him in one of the isolation chambers for days below the Wheel of Thought. They told everyone he had lost his mind. When he came out, days later, his face was pale. They had used the subjoia on him."

"What's that?"

"It's a serum that makes you detect only the worst kinds of thoughts, anamatis from the Mazag. When you tune into another's thoughts, you just feel terrible inside. You feel only fear, anger, and grief. You feel as if you are in a never-ending spiral of fear and anxiety, an emotion worse than anything you can imagine. It's the worst kind of pain you can cause an ajnir. Not even physical pain is so bad."

Naria rubbed her porcelain-white hands across her brows once and sighed. Nadan could tell she was experiencing a kind of vicarious agony herself. She had obviously tuned into Fadakoa's mind after the event and seen what horrors lay inside. Nadan sensed it was an angst, a grief that was somehow linked to Mazag, as if all the world's travails trickled out of that one place. But whereas he had been an impermanent observer in that world, Fadakoa had had his mind opened to that plane of reality in a constant, unrelenting stream.

"I don't understand why they would want to keep reports about the uriel so suppressed," said Nadan.

The snowfall around them was starting to ebb. A man with a skiff plowed silently through the street, sweeping the street with an enormous mechanical broom connected to his arm.

"It has to do with the messages from the uriel," said Naria. "Many seem like nonsense and riddles. But others have reported other messages. Some of the messages contradict the teachings of the Order, a fact that caused the Order to become more concerned. A uriel told Fadakoa he should speak out on this to the Order."

For the first time, Nadan realized it. He wondered that he had been so blind all this time, all those hours walking among those ancient halls inside the Order. He had been so entranced by Surya's sweeping mannerisms and affluence that the realization had eluded him. The Order, like the corporations of Valyna, was no longer connected to Dinjin. It had become one more power-hungry mechanism, one more cog in the self-serving wheels that churned ceaselessly in this city's core being. All he had seen that day confirmed this opinion, as he recycled all the events of that day through his mind. The classes in the Wheel of Thought's sub-surface lair, which he had witnessed hours ago, were not directed to some higher aim but, rather, to the Order's own prominence. He sensed that there was some influence of the Mazag meandering through those halls, that crypt, and the Quenna that he had been unable to detect before.

Naria seemed to sense his thoughts. "The Order has drifted, I know," she said with a downcast air. "I've often wished to leave. But I would not know where to go."

The snow fell heavier again for a moment, and the wind picked up along the street, almost whisking the veil off their heads. Nadan reached up and held it firmly over them both. "You should come with me," said Nadan. It was a sudden instinct, but, as soon he said it, he knew it was the right thing to say. "I'm going to Kira Mandi soon. We can go, with as many of your friends as you like."

Naria seemed puzzled. Nadan felt her thoughts moving skillfully through the vast shores of the Watching. "But how would we get there?" Naria said, doubtfully. "I sense that decision is right, but my mind cannot see how to do it."

"I have been working in the mines," said Nadan. "I've saved up enough. I will have enough shortly to buy a skiff. We can use that to get across the desert."

At that moment, voices echoed off the buildings in the street. The sounds arose from a group of children, playing and throwing snow at each other on the street. Their shapes, barely discernible in the darkness, flitted like dancing shadows in the mist.

"I have to go," Naria said.

"Will you come with us?" asked Nadan.

"Who is us?" she asked.

"Me and my friend, Ranum," he said.

"I do not know," she said. "Too much is going on inside my head. I can't think right now."

The children were now closer. Their voices would whisper and then suddenly shout in the still air. A worried look suddenly stole across Naria's expression, almost as if she were seeing a ghost inside her thoughts. "I must go," she said. "I will find you later."

Throwing her hood over her red hair, she turned and disappeared into the darkening snow-fall. Nadan stood for a moment, peering into the blackness and crisp air where she had disappeared from sight. The children were so close to him now that he could see the mist from their breath in the air. They were laughing, speaking in Valynan. Nadan didn't understand their words, but they sounded as if they were bantering insults. He turned before they caught sight of him and moved along the street.

When he arrived at his kaaraadruun hut, he heated a spice drink over a heat globe and then lay down on his bed, sipping it reflectively. The snow outside had stopped. He opened the window and looked out. A stillness hung over the city, like a vacant, dazed dream. It was as if the air was holding its breath with some suppressed intention; there was a foreboding feeling, a sense of imminence.

As soon as he turned around and closed the window, he was faced with the materialization of that feeling. It was a uriel. Whether it was the same as the one that had visited him in Simkada months ago, he wasn't sure, but it looked almost identical.

Its arms were light tentacles, writhing in and out of his vision, like pulsating signal lights on a dark horizon. The air it moved in seemed to ripple, like a heat wave over the desert.

At that moment, Nadan suddenly remembered the strange phrase the creature had told him all those months ago: *The power from without is the wind.*

He suddenly saw that the riddle had been predictive, an insight that he had only realized just now, when he was here in Valyna. The being drew closer to him, and Nadan felt the hair on his head stand up in fear. But the fear quickly passed. The creature was so kind it could have melted the fear of a quaking child.

Amidst the vagaries . . . not a drop . . . ocean of life . . . the ocean . . . transcend the ocean.

The being's last phrase skittered away in the air, like pebbles on a walkway. Nadan was having more difficulty understanding the words than before. The being seemed to sense his uncertainty and moved closer to him; the uriel's invisible face created a humming sensation in the air in front of his eyes.

The beneath-me realm is clouding, it said.

It reached out with its phantom-like hand and plunged its fingers into his head. Nadan felt it cleaning the channels of his awareness again, extricating the dross of fear and worry from his mind. When the being removed its hand again, he again felt that same warm peace inundating his thoughts that he had felt that night when the being first visited him in Simkada.

What is your name? he telepathed to the creature.

Where I come from, names are prisons, it replied. Nadan felt suddenly that he could communicate with the being much more clearly now.

And where do you come from? said Nadan.

The being started vibrating warmly in the air. Nadan had the distinct impression it was chuckling.

Location means nothing, it said finally. The being's form seemed to weaken, and its communications became splotchy again. *Kira Mandi . . . your home.*

The creature glimmered and rippled for a moment and then moved backward in the room, floating up against the upper wall and chandelier lumin-globe. It sparkled, writhed, and twisted, then disappeared into the wall.

Nadan sensed the uriel had gone for the time being and wouldn't be back for a while. He lay down on his bed, thinking: *Why did the being say Kira Mandi is my home?* He drifted off to sleep, still pondering the question, but reaching no satisfying conclusion.

Chapter 11

Escape from the City

The next day, Nadan woke late. He got up as quickly as he could, dressed, and went to meet Surya at the Quenna headquarters. He intended to leave soon for Kira Mandi, but he still was interested in learning more about the Quenna and the Wheel of Thought's underground lair. When he reached the headquarters, the same servant led him up the spiraling steps to the vast chamber, where the Valynan businessman sat everyday on his crimson cushions, weighing major decisions about the Quenna.

The day was warm outside, and the large doors at the far end of the hall were swung open wide, so that the sunlight from the Light Star beamed into the vast luxury chamber. Outside in the courtyard, light leapt about in a fountain with a gold figure-eight symbol in its center. Surya led him outdoors through the open doors of the hall, which looked more like gates to a city than actual doors.

When Nadan's eyes adjusted to the light, he saw dense rows of trees spanning several acres across a flat plain: pafnegu, palm, galan, Kurieme, and a host of other varieties he had never seen before. He had never seen so many trees. Simkada had only one small forest on the western outskirts of the city and a few scattered trees lining the major thoroughfares.

"Although the Quenna's main commodity is acron, we do specialize in other things as well," said Surya. His normally restrained features could barely suppress his immense pride at the sight before him. "Tell me, Nadan, have you read much about Valyna?"

"Yes, on occasion," said Nadan.

"Then you must have read of the great Dewar Forest of the olden days, in the pre-futuristic era?" said Surya.

"Of course." Nadan remembered that the Dewar Forest had once spanned most of what was now Valyna. Wars, famines, and mining operations from Valyna had mostly decimated the forest thousands of years ago.

The proud expression grew brighter on Surya's face. "This nursery will be the first seeds of rebuilding that once-great forest," he said.

"That is a noble aim," said Nadan.

He looked out across the nursery again. The snow from the night before was weighing down heavily on the branches and boughs of many of the trees. As he looked, one branch, glistening in the sunlight, dipped, and the snow resting on it fell heavily, thudding on the turf. It was an enjoyable sight, one that made his soul relax after his tense conversations with Naria the night before. As he looked over at Surya's face, it seemed the man was also enjoying the scene, but in a different way. The Valynan's face seemed to be inscribed with plans, strategies, and a subdued sense of conquest that was not unlike a general's love of glory. Nadan sensed this place was more than an enjoyable sight for him; it meant political favor, the won hearts and minds of the masses.

Again, Nadan had the same sense that Surya was concealing his fears, worries, and griefs beneath a layer of perceptible social enjoyment. The thought strengthened his intentions to leave for Kira Mandi, but, at the same time, the man's stale sense of enjoyment evoked a sense of disappointment in Nadan's heart. At that moment, Nadan vowed he would never become part of that world himself.

Nadan talked with the ajnir for a few more hours, and then he left to return to his kaaraadruun hut, where he met Ranum. His friend was sitting in a stone chair, hunched over a table in the dining chamber, his golden hair disheveled.

"You mean to go," said Ranum. His voice was noticeably upset.

"Yes, I meant to talk to you now about it," replied Nadan, coolly.

He searched his friend's thoughts for a few seconds. He could tell that his friend did not want to leave the city. Ranum had grown to love the place more than he. Ranum was more of a Valynan than a Simkadan. His socially outgoing ways had never meshed with the reservations of the Simkadan people. Here he had found others who thought like him. But there was also something more: Nadan was receiving mental images of a girl's face, with a large mole on her cheek, flowing brown hair, and pale skin. The girl lived down the street from them.

"You want to stay because of the girl, Gueala," said Nadan, at length.

"I do want to go with you, but I would also like to stay here for a while," he said. "I don't know what to do. It's tearing me up inside. I've never felt like this."

"You can stay, if you like," Nadan said. "It's your choice. I don't think I will be gone more than a few months. If I am, perhaps you can come then. You could also try to bring Gueala with us."

"It is a dangerous journey," said Ranum ruefully, staring at his wrist gauge moodily. "Perhaps you could get in trouble. Perhaps the skiff will break down. You were never good with fixing machines. Gueala doesn't want to leave the city. She's afraid of Kira Mandi, being a Valynan."

"I may have others along with me."

Nadan explained to him his meeting with Naria, as well as his journey into the bowels of the Wheel of Thought. Ranum's jaw dropped open in fascination, as Nadan relayed the story about encountering Manalk through the use of the arthanti. When he heard the news about Naria possibly fleeing with him, Ranum's face brightened somewhat.

"That makes me feel better," he said, finally. But still he did not say whether he would go on the journey or not.

They ate dinner together quietly that night. Ranum seemed ill. His face was a greenish hue, and when he spoke, his voice was hoarse. After they had eaten, Ranum went to lie down on his bed. Nadan settled into reading the city's newspaper and reading ads for ant-gravity skiffs. He counted up his money and found that he had just enough, with some help from Ranum, to buy one of the better models.

While he was doing this, he suddenly heard a crash against the wall, as if someone had thrown a large stone against the wall of the hut. He walked into Ranum's chamber and his friend was crouched down on the floor, gripping a stone statue of a Valynan deity, Quigga, in his left hand.

"Look," he said.

Ranum held up the small object in his hand.

Nadan took out his telescoping glasses from his robe, placed them on his nose, and examined it closer, zeroing in the lenses. It was a small silver metal ball with a ring of tiny glass lenses surrounding its diameter. The ball was emanating a green static.

"It's a spy orb," said Ranum. His voice was tremulous with excitement, shaded with fear. "I've read about these before. They use them in Valyna. Someone must be very interested in our conversations. Luckily, I destroyed it. It will never bring a message back to its owner now. I saw it hovering over me when I was dozing off and hit it quickly with this." He pointed to the statue he had doubled as a club.

Ranum returned the statue to the marble console near his cot, then looked at the surveillance device again in his hand.

"But who would want to know what we are talking about?" he said.

"I think we can assume it's someone in the Wheel of Thought, maybe even Sakr Ka," said Nadan.

He was wondering how many conversations they had overheard in that hut over the last few months. He and Ranum had talked many times of their plans to leave for Kira Mandi. The Wheel of Thought must know of that. It also must know about his interest in the uriel and his experience back in Simkada. He and Ranum had talked often of that, debating the messages and riddles of the being far into the night sometimes.

"At least they don't know of my plans to leave soon," said Nadan. "Or I do not sense that they do. I think this means I must leave quickly, tonight or tomorrow if possible."

"I must go with you, then," said Ranum.

"No, you can stay here, as I said."

"No, I cannot stay here now. That's obvious. The Order is watching my every move."

Ranum flung the metal spy object onto the floor. It splintered into hundreds of pieces.

So it was decided. Ranum packed their belongings, while Nadan went out into the markets to buy an anti-gravity skiff. He bought the model he had been looking for at one of the Drogham markets and drove it slowly back to their kaaraadruun hut. It was a silverish, sleek machine with a black and gold stripe running down the side. The skiff was easier to drive than Nadan had expected, although he steered it more cautiously through the streets than did the other drivers of the skiffs about him. He had only driven a skiff on rare occasions.

When he had parked the vehicle by their kaaraadruun hut, they loaded up their baggage and clothes for their journey. Ranum wanted to bring the many clothes and possessions they had acquired in the city, but Nadan forced him to pare down their belongings. He knew they would need extra space for Naria. As they were storing the things in the skiff, Nadan was wondering how he would contact Naria again. She had not told him where she lived.

Even as he had the thought, a reddish orb zig-zagged through the street and hovered in front of his eyelid. Ranum stared, as it circled his head playfully and moved close to his ear.

We are leaving soon, Nadan telepathed.

I know, I will come. I will find you soon. The voice from the orb conveyed the childlike presence of Naria, but something about her mind felt slightly different, more anxious and worried.

They waited for several minutes on the street, but Naria didn't come. As they were waiting, Nadan noticed something like a black cloud, hovering over the street.

"What do you think that is?" he asked Ranum.

By the time Ranum had looked, the black cloud had formed into an orb of some sort and was jumping and dancing about in the air. Ranum stepped toward it but, after he had taken a few steps, the charcoal-colored orb disappeared into the wall.

Even as it vanished, Naria appeared on the street, emerging from a narrow alleyway between two kaaraadruun huts. She was carrying a small bundle of clothes, tightly rolled, in her left arm. When she got closer to Nadan, he could see her eyes were downcast.

"I have never left the city even once," she said.

"It's not so bad," said Nadan, comfortingly. "You will feel freer out there. The Wheel of Thought won't be there."

After he took her bundle of belongings and set them inside the anti-gravity skiff, Ranum ignited the engine. The vehicle sputtered and then emitted a slow, guttural sound that reverberated along the streetscape. The engine sound reduced itself to the tone of a slow, soft wind through the trees. Nadan and Naria both climbed aboard.

"Did you see that black thing?" Nadan asked Naria.

"No."

"It felt like a telepath orb, but it was black. It felt malevolent."

Naria shrugged but said nothing. Nadan could tell her mind was turned elsewhere, straying across the kaaraadruun huts and smokestacks and the distant image of the translucent towers against the gray skyline. She was hiding her face. It was as if she was absorbing the last images of this city for her permanent memory; Nadan knew she meant never to return to her homeland again.

"You know this is the right thing," he said.

"Yes, I know," she said softly, but still sadly.

Ranum engaged the lever of the skiff, and the vehicle jolted forward quickly. They were soon skimming along the stones of the street. A fog, which often crept across the city from the ocean, hung over the buildings, enshrouding them in a layer of mystery. The huts, covered in melting snow, moved by like dream patterns.

Chapter 12

The Anatami

They moved through the gates of the city swiftly. Once they were out, Ranum maneuvered the skiff to the west, banking it on its side, so that Naria and Nadan had to clutch the sides of the skiff to stay balanced. Ranum was the most expert of the three with operating skiffs; he had used them back in Simkada, when he used to work for the city's gardening operations.

They were now moving down a shallow rut, which had been carved out for hundreds of years by skiffs and cargo vehicles that had shuttled goods from Valyna to Kira Mandi. The road, known in Valyna as the Anatami Road, was the second major artery, besides the Quantan Way that fed in and out of the city. A third highway, known as the Volik, led around the Arwanu Sea, but Nadan had never been to it.

They passed a chain of cargo-skiff operators who had stopped near the side of the highway. They were leaning against their vehicles in the dusk and drinking clinus from their canteens. With their helmets thrown back on their shoulders and the sunlight behind them, they looked almost like Valynan warriors in the dark. None of the skiffs were moving in the night, and they passed none as they swept along the road.

In a few minutes, they reached the open desert, which stretched out like a perfectly flattened palm on all sides. The soothing desert wind on his face felt liberating to Nadan, after a month spent in the densely populated environment of Valyna. The breeze seemed to waft away the intricacies of his existence and fling them back into the dark, web-like world of endless strategy and opaque political intrigue that he was leaving. The inner joy, the simplicity, of pure being was finally returning to him, a sense of wild, crazed freedom that seemed mirrored in the empty, barren landscape around him. He had never seen emptiness as beautiful before, but, now, he saw that it was the ultimate beauty. He needed to worry about nothing. Naria seemed to sense his mood. Her face was uplifted. In the short time he had known her, he had not seen her eyes so bright and radiant.

The moon came out over the desert, and it deepened the wild sense of liberation they felt. They were moving past small tree-like shrubs that loomed up in the lumin-lights that wavered on the front of their skiff.

They traveled all night, not stopping once. Ranum and Nadan alternated over the controls of the vehicle throughout the night, sleeping in turns in the back of the skiff. Naria fell asleep on a small, sheltered bunk in the back of the vehicle. Ranum had wanted to stop late in the night, but Nadan warned against it. He was almost certain that the Wheel of Thought knew of their flight already, and he wasn't certain if members of the Order would give chase.

When the sun rose over the lip of the horizon ahead of them that morning, they finally saw what he had feared most. As they looked back, amidst the eddies of golden sand that lashed up in their swath, they saw several small shapes just behind them, their images rippling back and forth in the heat waves of dawn.

"Do you think it's the Order?" asked Ranum.

Nadan didn't reply but pulled out his telescoping glasses from his robe pocket. He placed them on the end of his nose and adjusted the lenses to their maximum length visibility setting.

"Yes, it's Valynan warriors," he said calmly, after a moment. "I knew they were behind us."

Naria lifted her head up, shaking her long auburn hair as she lay on the bench. She had been sleeping, but the conversation had awoken her.

"They could be traveling to Kira Mandi, like us," she said.

"No, the Valyna military has withdrawn from the borders of Kira Mandi," said Nadan, taking off his glasses. "I read the news back in the city. No warriors from either side are crossing this far into the desert because of the recent treaty. I think we must assume they are after us, unless their plans are to break the peace or deliver a message to Kira Mandi. There are hidden monitors installed in the sands after they get a certain distance from Kira Mandi, which will tell them of any infractions further up along this road. Somewhere around the Dholan sand dunes. I wonder if they will dare to cross the border."

Together, he and Naria stretched out their thoughts to the distant shapes. The murky mental cloud that deflected their thoughts was becoming a familiar sensation for Nadan.

"If they are using veils, then that must mean they are from the Wheel of Thought," deducted Naria, dejectedly.

"Ranum, are we going as fast as we can go?" asked Nadan.

The skiff rattled loudly for a moment, as Ranum pushed the throttle of the skiff, and they skimmed, serenely and silently, over the surface of the beaten rut of a road. The dust kicking up behind them now almost completely blocked their view of the skiffs in their rear. It was now early morning, and the sun was blazing down on their heads with pitiless attention. The intermittent habitat that had bordered the road for miles now gave way to a bumpy, lifeless terrain that undulated in small, rippling knolls. The road began arcing through the landscape, and Ranum had to slow the skiff several times to keep it on the curving path. Then, suddenly, the hills dropped away, and they were in a desolate, flat desert again, but this time with no trees or shrubs in sight anywhere. The area was barren and bleak, and the sand was a different color: reddish-coral. The wind had also picked up and was now howling across their faces, flinging up the dirt and sand into their teary eyes.

Together, Nadan and Naria mounted the canopy over the skiff to block the wind. When they had finished, they looked back, peering through a small round glass portal at the base of the skiff's tail.

"They have gained on us," said Naria, anxiously.

"It's as I thought," said Ranum. "The warriors all have special skiffs that can outrun any of the ones you can buy in the markets so as to ensure no one can outpace the city's military."

"What can we do?" said Naria. Her voice was almost frantic.

Ranum said nothing but turned his eyes forward, stonily staring into the desert land ahead.

Naria didn't speak her fears outwardly, but Nadan knew what she was thinking: Her mind was skittering frenetically over the dark, fractured being of her friend who had talked of the uriel. Would the Wheel of Thought use the subjoia, the deadly mind serum, on them if they were caught? Naria kept clasping her knees on the bench, while they all fell silent. Nadan stooped down every few minutes to check the portal. The red shapes were growing steadily larger in the window. But suddenly, the pursuing craft slowed and drifted back, then turned and disappeared into the shallow knolls that they had just emerged from.

"They've gone," said Nadan, elated. "They've turned around."

Naria unclasped her legs and looked out back through the portal. Nadan sensed that the fear of the serum and the grotesque imagery of the prison, deep in the bowels of the Order, had temporarily vanished from Naria's thoughts. The radiant liberation her mind had experienced the night before flooded back into her consciousness, like a thawing stream in springtime.

Nadan, too, felt his pounding heart slowing, and his muscles relaxing.

"I don't understand why they turned back," said Ranum. "They could have easily overtaken us. The Dholan Dunes aren't for a mile or so."

He slowed the skiff down and resumed the normal cruising speed. They had run from the Valynan warriors for almost an entire day, and the sun was now dipping below the horizon. The last remaining rays of sunlight blazed in their eyes ahead of them, but, through the glare they could see sand mounds rising, casting elongated shadows on the sand, which had now transformed from crimson-coral to a golden whitish hue.

When they reached the mounds, Ranum slowed the skiff and Nadan peeled off the canopy of the vehicle.

"These are the Dholan Dunes," said Ranum. "These warriors will be much less inclined to capture us here."

"I'm not certain, but I sense you are right," said Nadan.

Ranum brought the vehicle to a full halt along a shallow curve in the road, and they all got out and stretched their legs in the bright, luminescent sand. Ranum and Nadan together worked on setting up the tent for the evening. An hour later, after they had finished setting it up, they stretched out next to a heat-globe they had mounted in a large indentation in the sand and munched on roasted vegetables and pieces of pafnegu bread.

As they were eating, they slowly became aware of a sound like digging in the sand near them in the darkness. Nadan got up and walked over to the lumin-globe, turning the switch to maximize the light output. As the yellow light shot out in the desert, they saw what had made the sound. It was a small rodent or animal, jumping back and forth in the turf, sending up a cloud of sand around it.

They remained motionless, while the creature kicked around a circle in the sand with its hind paws. It almost seemed to be dancing or performing some sort of ritual.

Nadan had never seen anything like this animal before, even in pictures he had studied back in the crypts in Simkada. The creature seemed to have the body of a large white rodent, but its upper abdomen was similar to that of a cat. Its features were strange, too, almost a mix between a lion and a tiny horse. But the strangest part of it was the long, white tentacle that protruded from the back of its skull and danced around in the air, like a senseless whip, as it jumped around near them.

Suddenly, it stopped kicking its legs in the sand and looked Nadan directly in the eyes, as if it had known all along that he had been watching. Its eyes were noble and intelligent, like windows into a primordial realm. It seemed both human and anciently wild. Even as Nadan stared into those unusual eyes, he knew the animal was telepathic.

Follow me, it telepathed into his mind.

It was a clear communication, as clear as Manalk's. Nadan took a step back in the sand and felt the wind blowing along his face, as if in slow motion.

"Did you feel that?" he whispered to Ranum. "It telepathed."

Ranum nodded but said nothing. His face was drawn with a kind of fear but also intrigued. He was leaning against the back of the skiff, with a clay mug between his palms, the light glaring off his golden hair. Naria sat next to him, staring, her face placid, almost as if she wasn't surprised that the animal was telepathic.

The creature moved closer to Nadan, only a few feet away, and began purring in a strange way. It was obviously less afraid than they were.

"Should we do what it asks?" asked Nadan.

"It is your choice," said Ranum, ambiguously. "It seems to like you."

Naria moved toward the creature with her hand extended.

"It's an omisat," she said. "Not many around Valyna, but I knew one there."

"What is that?" asked Nadan.

"Telepathic animals. They have one at the Quenna, a parrot named Sadu. Yet, I feel this one is higher, more intelligent, more aware somehow, though." Her face was mottled, confused. "It is a strange voice, but it means well, I think," she added, after a moment's thought.

Nadan moved over to the creature slowly, in a crouching position. Even as he leaned forward to pet it, it suddenly jumped back into the darkness again, flipping its white tentacle toward him. He sensed it wasn't so much fear in the animal; moreso, it was several layers of reactions that were too deep for him to immediately intuit.

I cannot be touched by you, said the creature, *or else I would shed this form.*

What are you? said Nadan back.

I can be so many things, not unlike you, it said.

The creature stood still, as the heat-globe near their skiff let out a huge puff of steam next to them. Then, it turned and disappeared into the darkness, beyond one of the windswept sand hills.

Nadan got up from his sitting position and looked at both his friends.

"Let's follow it," he said. "I don't sense it is being deceptive."

Nadan waved his hand forward, and Ranum and Naria both fell in behind him, treading lightly in the sand. The moon was now showing above the horizon in front of them, and the sand below their feet was almost pale white in its light. Nadan almost felt like he was again on the sandy shores of the Arwanu Sea, but the sound of surf was replaced by the sighing of the desert breeze through the small cacti and shrubs that surrounded them. Everywhere about their feet, lizards and small snakes were darting about through the vegetation. Ahead of them, the creature's tentacle wiggled in the air at an upright position every few minutes, as if using it to help them keep sight of itself.

They had walked nearly a mile through the dunes, when the ground dropped off into a sheer basin that opened up suddenly at their feet. When Nadan came over the edge of it, he immediately saw a large bonfire at the bottom of the small valley. Chanting could be heard in the distance, and dark shapes flitted around it, some dancing, others still.

Nadan had half-suspected some scene such as this, even as he had begun to follow the strange animal. The words from the Drogham chief back in the desert all those months ago echoed in his ears again: *The Anatami are once again on the desert*. It is said the people could converse with animals. He wondered: *Could they speak with animals using an ajnir-like telepathy?* It seemed a logical conclusion, if the fable was true.

He looked to his side and saw Naria there, in her green, flowing gown in the darkness beside him. He couldn't see her expression in the dim light, but he could feel her mind brimming with excitement and energy.

"This can't be . . ." she said, after a moment, sensing his mind.

"Yes, it is the Anatami," said Nadan.

"But they are said to have died out hundreds of years ago," she said.

"I thought so too," he said. "We met a Drogham chief outside Simkada, who told us the ancient tribe still lived on the desert."

They walked further down the embankment, which was so steep they partially slid down it. By this time, the strange creature had already passed beyond and into the circle of people around the fire. It was nodding its head, seeming to converse silently with one of the tribal members. As they approached, a man stepped out of the circle to greet them.

With the light from the fire against his back, none of them could discern the man's features. But his shape was tall and thin, and he moved like a desert animal. He was carrying a small spear in his left hand, which he drove into the ground in front of him. As soon as he did, all talking around the fire ceased, and a stillness fell in the air. The figures all turned toward the three strangers. Nadan felt their thoughts bearing down upon him with a sense of dismay. In that brief instant, he sensed the soul of this people, the same as he had when he had first walked into the gates of Valyna. The feeling was simple and primordial; the awareness seemed woven together, interwoven with the earth itself. He saw endless years spent under the stars and sun, blended together, heedless of the meanderings and machinations of civilization.

The man standing in front of them addressed them in the common tongue. "My name is Shakul," he said. "I do not know why Laki has asked me to speak with you. Normally, we remain hidden from anyone from the three cities. But she is our mentor and our chief. If we challenge her, we might as well challenge the god of air and earth itself, for she is one with it in herself."

He waved with his hand toward the fire where the strange creature had been, but it had disappeared into the blackness. He had spoken in a perfect Valynan accent, which seemed to Nadan a strange contrast to the setting.

"My name is Nadan, and these are my two companions, Ranum and Naria," he said. "We are traveling to Kira Mandi. We were led here by that strange animal. Is this the one you call Laki?"

"It is," said the man, in a peculiar way.

"What sort of animal is it? We were confused. It is like nothing I have ever seen before." Nadan hesitated about saying more. He didn't know if the man understood telepathing.

"Laki has many shapes, and she assumes them at will," Shakul said. "We never know how she will appear to us next. She often assumes that form you witnessed, however. It suits our desert environment well."

"How is it that you speak so fluently the Valynan speech, if you are born as an Anatami?"

"I can see that you have not been able to see my face."

The man moved to Nadan's side and faced the fire. The dancing circle of tribal folk turned as he did and let out a long, slow guttural sound that shivered in the darkness. Drums around them began to throb in the darkness, off in the far corner of the encampment. As Shakul turned to face the fire, Nadan could see that his skin was pallid and white, unlike the dark-skinned Anatami Nadan had seen in history books.

"I am a Valynan by birth, but I came to join the Anatami many sun rotations ago to become one of them," he said. "They accept anyone who will join and accept their manner of living as one of their own family: that is, if Laki permits them to find them."

"And why did you wish to leave Valyna?" asked Naria. She had appeared without a sound at his side.

Shakul's eyes drifted over the fire to the red moon, Kindri, hanging crescent shaped on the western horizon. Nadan peered into his mind, perceiving that he was thinking about a Valynan woman, someone he had been in love with many years ago.

"I came because I had grown ashamed of my city and its wars," he said, despondently. "I was once a Valynan soldier in the Mandian War, but I defected during one of the desert battles and found the Anatami. It was a difficult life at first, living with no technology, but I've grown accustomed to it."

The crowd of Anatami suddenly cheered and rattled their spears, and their songs broke loose loudly into a deafening chant. Nadan and Shakul could no longer speak. Shakul turned to join the fray of warriors, thumping his spear on the ground in unison with the others. The words sounded like this: *tunal abul shanka muna guinta.*

"Means a warrior's death is nothing in the Cosmic Sphere, what we call Laki's world," explained Shakul, coming back to join them after a minute or so. Nadan could sense he was aroused and enlivened by the song, but beneath it, he was worried and anxious.

"Sounds like a battle song," remarked Ranum.

"I'm not supposed to tell you, but we are preparing for a fight tomorrow," Shakul said. "Valyna is taking our land to the east, and we will join our other brothers for a stand there."

"How many of the Anatami are left?" asked Ranum. "Why is it that we had been told that your people had gone extinct?"

"We number in the low thousands," said Shakul. "As for your second question, I'm not sure why that fable is told in your lands to the south. Valyna once believed the Anatami were extinct, too. The tribe has hidden itself carefully from the world for years. It wasn't until Hajui, the Valynan explorer, trekked across the Kiopic Desert a decade ago that he rediscovered that the Anatami still existed. Kira Mandi has always laid claim over the desert but has allowed the Anatami to coexist with their authority peacefully. But when Valyna discovered acron reservoirs beneath this soil, they sought to claim the land from Mandi. When Mandi learned of the land's value, they too sought to control the land. Both cities, but especially Valyna, are trying to push us out of these lands."

"It is interesting that the war has been ongoing for nine years, but I never knew it was over acron," said Ranum. "You number so few. Do you have any hope?"

Shakul's eyes fell. He watched the dark shapes scattering into the darkness around them for a moment. They moved completely silently, like shadows across the desert. When he finally spoke, it was in a low voice. "I know many would stay until they die," he whispered. "But Laki spoke to me two suns ago. She said, if the battle is not won tomorrow, she will tell us all to move north and cede our lands to the Valynans. I cannot say what her reasoning is. I'm certain that would draw protests from the tribe."

Nadan wondered if Laki had assumed a human form when she spoke to him. He opened his mouth to ask the question, but a hoot like an owl sounded in the air near them, and he shut it quickly.

"I'm needed," said Shakul. "We are drawing up plans, and I am to lead the assault tomorrow, since I understand Valyna warfare."

He waved his hand at them, then said: "I enjoyed speaking with you. It has been long since I spoke the common tongue with someone."

"Where is Laki now?" said Nadan. "I wish to speak with her again."

"Laki is wild, like the lizard in the desert," said Shakul. "She comes and goes like the wind. You cannot see where or why she comes."

With these enigmatic words, Shakul turned and disappeared into the darkness. Nadan suddenly realized that they would have to take the initiative to find some place to sleep for the night.

"It is a warm night," said Ranum, seeming to read his mind. "I don't think we need to go back to the skiff. We can just sleep here, I say."

They searched around the area, which was now deserted, except for a few Anatami at the top of the embankment. Soon they found a large, oval indentation in the sand, where they spread out their robes and lay on top of them, bare limbed except for their undergarments. The Kindri moon was now high above the western horizon line and seemed to smile upon their bodies, delightfully. Nadan searched out with his thoughts for Laki but couldn't find her in the immediate area. But he sensed somehow she was pleased this night, wherever she was.

Soon, he drifted off to sleep. He slipped into a dream, in which he was back in Valyna, back inside the Wheel of Thought headquarters. People whom he knew were not ajnir were walking about the Wheel of Thought freely, looking inside the somber chambers with smiles and laughs written on their faces. Nadan felt cramped and exposed, as if under a critical and judgmental public lens. As he walked down the corridor, he met a small girl, with black hair and dark features, whose eyes fixed on his with lurid intensity. A sudden clarity came to the dream, so that he actually became aware that he was dreaming. With a conscious effort, he reached out to touch the girl's face, but, at that moment, he awoke and saw that the same girl in his dream was standing in front of him. The moon was low on the horizon over the desert, and the light played in her dark hair, flitting about in the breeze. He didn't feel frightened because he knew that this was Laki herself, in a different form.

"When you bring the world back to itself, we will be waiting for you in Gargol," she said, in the common tongue.

"I do not understand what you mean, child," he said, getting up from the sand.

"Never mind," she said, coolly. "You will understand when it is the right time. But I am not a child, at least by your standards. I am three hundred years old and still I have not reached adulthood."

She turned away from him and suddenly fell on the ground, twisting and writhing. Nadan stared, as she changed shape before his eyes into the strange creature they had followed before, with its noble face and white tentacle protruding from its head. The creature got up and stared at him, eyes playful and blissful, before plunging back into the darkness. Nadan got the sense he should not pursue her.

Nadan lay back on the sand, wondering: *What is Gargol?* He had studied numerous maps of Urshan

Dai throughout his life, but he had never seen or heard of the place mentioned. He soon fell asleep again. He awoke the next morning with Shakul standing over him. The man's face was painted in gold and black and crimson stripes, with a strange lizard form painted on the back of his bald scalp.

"We leave soon for battle," he said. "I come to wish you well before we leave, Nadan. Your friends have already left. They will meet you at the skiff, they said."

Nadan looked around and saw that Naria and Ranum had both disappeared; their robes were gone from the sand. Black shapes of Anatami, also painted in the same gold and charcoal colors, shifted to and fro beyond Shakul's pallid form.

Nadan got up from the sand and said: "Laki appeared to me last night and spoke of a place called Gargol. Do you know the meaning of the word?"

"It is a word that is difficult to put in the common tongue," said Shakul. "But it means the civilized world. It is the place of technology, but more essentially, it means the place where your true leaders are unrecognized or hidden from view. They are consigned to living in your world in disguise."

Nadan now began to understand what Laki meant, but still he wondered what a strange contrast to meet that otherwordly, mythical child in a place like Simkada or Valyna. He feared they might just imprison her and study her in some way and not let her roam free, as she did in the desert.

Even as he thought about this, a shout rose up from behind one of the sand dunes to the west of them. Shakul immediately ran to the top of the dune, with Nadan trailing behind him. When Nadan pulled up behind Shakul at the top of the ridge, the man turned quickly and pressed his hand against his chest, pushing him back down the hill.

"Danger," he hissed. "The soldiers must have followed your tracks to our encampment."

Nadan crouched in the shadows, listening to the sound of Valynan gun arrows plunking off the metal shields of the tribe's warriors and the occasional shout from one of the men. Shakul remained crouched at the top of the dune's ridge, peering over the lip, like a cat waiting to pounce. Suddenly, after a minute or so, he mounted the ridge and with a yell, threw his long spear. Nadan heard it plunk against the metal of an anti-gravity skiff and after that, he saw arrows from the Valynan ship whizzing over the sand dune as the soldiers took aim at Shakul, who had quickly returned to where Nadan was sitting. The man was mumbling to himself in the Anatami language, murmuring as if reciting some chant or mantra to himself.

Nadan rose to his feet and walked to the ridge and peered over the edge, as Shakul disappeared around the other side of the dune. Below him, he could see two anti-gravity skiffs, leaping about in the air, spraying arrows left and right from guns below the floor of their ships. Two Valynan warriors were on each of the skiffs, but below them a third skiff rested battered and broken on the turf, with two other warriors lying face down in the sand nearby. Next to them lay an Anatami warrior, his body peppered with skiff darts. Blood oozed through the sand and ran like thick water down the gully between the two sand dunes.

A loud cry went up in the air from all the Anatami, and Nadan shuddered at the sight, as the warriors made a sudden blitz charge on the soldiers, hemming them in and running at them from all sides over the ridges of the dunes. The sound of metal and wood clashed furiously in the air; one, then two Anatami fell, arrows from the ships piercing their eyes and skulls and chests. Then, the tribal warriors were upon them, knocking the soldiers off the skiffs with their spears. Close to them, a large, bulky Anatami warrior, with gold paint and sand covering his body for camouflage, thrust a Valynan soldier to the ground with his long spear. The fallen soldier leaned up and shot his arrow gun toward the Anatami's thigh, but the Anatami was too quick. With an agile movement, he swiftly lifted the man's helmet off his head, exposing his enemey's auburn long hair, tied in a ponytail. Even as the Anatami warrior raised his knife to the man's throat, Nadan turned his head and moved back down the embankment. He had never seen warfare before, and it turned his stomach to watch. He sat there on the embankment, listening to the weeping of Anatami women in the background as they rushed onto the small, sandy battlefield. Even as he sat there, he could sense the presence of the man who had just been killed near him; the man's soul seemed to flit in the atmosphere near the sand dune. He couldn't see the man's apparition, but he could feel his thoughts, as he angrily watched the scene, outside of his body, saying to himself: *It was always our land before.*

Then, the man's soul fled the battle scene and the physical universe, and Nadan was unable to detect his thoughts any longer.

Shakul reappeared at the top of the ridge, with a crying Anatami woman at his side. She was extremely thin, almost deathly emaciated, and had a necklace of bones around her chest which rattled, as she came up and struck Nadan across the chest with her hand. Shakul held her back, pulling her back onto the ridge, as she struggled to break free. She was speaking angrily at Nadan in her language and weeping. Shakul kept speaking softly to her, obviously trying to placate her anger.

"She is angry at you because they followed your tracks to this camp," Shakul said. "Her husband, Jkal, was killed in the attack." He kept speaking to her in her own language. Other warriors came up from behind her and pulled her back down the slope, away from the battle scene.

"I feel guilty," said Nadan. "I have done a great wrong without knowing it. Had I but known, I would not have come here."

Shakul picked up one of the bones that had fallen from the women's chest and placed it carefully in his pouch. He stood there for a moment, glancing reflectively at the horizon to the north where sand dunes etched the landscape like an undulating ocean. He was holding a white bandage against one of his arms, where a dart had grazed his shoulder. The desert had become quiet again, and a mysterious, lurid tranquility hung about it, except for the intermittent cry of Anatami women and men off in the distance.

"We were ill prepared for the attack," he said, dryly. "We have lost three of our warriors, and many more of us sustained wounds. But I for one do not blame you for what happened. It is not what I would have planned, but Laki led you here, and I aim my anger more at her for this attack. It's a tribal belief to never question the words of the elder child, but I for one am starting to question that. Two turns of the moon ago, we were ambushed by soldiers, and Laki never warned us, as she used to in the past. She always seems to have some plan we do not understand or see very easily. I do not know."

He shook his head, and ran his palms along his shoulder. "At least we shall have skiffs and weaponry to use from this battle," he said, after a moment. "That is the only good I can see from this. But I fear that some of the warriors will be angered with you. I will try to persuade them the best I can, but I think it is best, for your own safety, to leave now. They may think that you purposely led the soldiers here and will stop trusting you."

Shakul bowed low before him and performed the same hand gestures he had the night before. Nadan mirrored the gesture. Then, without another word, the Anatami man turned and disappeared over the ridge of the embankment, to a place nearby where he could hear the sound of weeping still biting the air.

Nadan made his way back to the place where they had slept. In a few minutes, he reached the skiff, where Ranum and Naria were sitting together. They explained that they had risen early and that when they heard the battle off in the distance, had taken cover in the distant dunes with some Anatami children.

"We need to go," said Nadan. "The warriors and the women are angered, thinking that we led the soldiers here. Shakul said they may cause trouble for us."

"It makes me feel terrible," said Naria, standing up. "But we had no way of knowing. Laki led us here."

"I know," said Nadan. "Shakul is on our side, and he plans to argue our case before the rest of the tribe. They may believe him, but for now, there might be some immediate backlash against us."

Together they all got on the skiff. Ranum ignited the machine, and soon they were zooming off over the sand, back to the Anatami Road. The paths of the soldier's skiffs were still clear in the sand, so they had no trouble finding their way back to the road. The Light Star was now at mid horizon, and the air was dry and hot. The three travelers were all quiet and depressed and didn't speak much as they whizzed along the desert. As they reached the road finally, Nadan spoke.

"I met Laki again last night, in a different form," he said. "Did you see her?"

"No," said Ranum. "But I heard someone whispering in my ear last night. When I awoke there was no one there. And I couldn't remember what the words said. It was strange. I've never had a dream like that before."

"I met a woman in a dream," Naria said. She was sitting in the back of the skiff, with a tan robe huddled around her for shade. "She told me many things about the place we were sleeping, but I can't remember them either."

Naria paused for a moment.

"This place is strange to me,' she said. "It almost feels like the Wheel of Thought headquarters, but more ancient and foreign."

Nadan looked at her sharply. He had been feeling the same thing, an emotion dormant beneath his conscious awareness, except that he hadn't clearly articulated the emotion to himself yet.

"I sense that too," he said. "There is something older, more primordial here. But I also sense some form of stagnation, similar to Simkada. It is as if the place is wrapped up inside itself, like a cocoon."

They moved on through the deep desert, the skiff bouncing slightly as they careened down the ancient highway. The distance across the desert seemed unimaginable in its flatness. It was bare and bleak, and the plant life that had sprinkled the landscape near the Anatami gathering had disappeared.

As the wind coursed through his ears, Nadan almost thought he could hear the sound of those same primordial drums that had throbbed in his ears last night. Then, in an instant, the sound was gone, dwindling into the vacant barrenness surrounding them.

Chapter 13

Kira Mandi

They passed quickly along the road that day, barely stopping except to stretch their legs and take short walks in the desert sand every few hours. They wanted to pass beyond the barren desert as quickly as possible. Its bleak sense of isolation weighed heavily on them; they passed no cargo skiffs along this stretch of the highway.

They continued to drive onward throughout the night, taking turns at operating the silver craft. At one point, Nadan was awakened by Naria, who had been steering for several hours. It was late in the night, almost morning, and the cool desert wind almost felt chilly.

"I saw a large bird flying up behind us," she said. "I'm not sure what it was, but it seemed odd behavior for a bird. It made no noise and flew steadily in the air, without weaving or banking."

Nadan rubbed his fingers through his hair, threw his blankets off, and looked back. He could see nothing behind the skiff now, amidst the dark clouds of sand eddying up in their wake. The sky was eerily empty; the stars were a profound white, and the constellations were crystalline. He got up and shook the sleep off himself, and took Naria's place at the helm of the craft. Naria took his spot on the bench where he had slept, curling up in the same soft wool blanket.

He drove for almost an hour, his senses gradually awakening, as dawn crept over the horizon, like a silent, luminous cat. First, the sky turned bluish over the landscape, then orange, then faintly reddish, as the Light Star gradually ascended. When he moved his head to look off to the south across the desert, he caught the glint of something silver in his peripheral vision. He turned quickly and saw a large orb hovering in the air behind him. As soon as he focused, however, the object turned and sped off to a distant corner of the horizon. He followed it with his eyes as it disappeared into the sun and billowing sand.

Naria woke a few minutes later, rubbing her white knuckles in her eye sockets.

"That bird you saw was no bird," said Nadan. "It was some kind of metal orb. I think it's tracking us. It may be from the Wheel of Thought."

Naria tossed the blanket to the floor of the skiff and turned to look back, as she tied her hair in two braids along her shoulders.

"Why would they still be interested in our movements?" she said, standing up and joining him in the cockpit.

"I was wondering if perhaps they were concerned we might tell the Mandian government of the Order's existence," said Nadan. "But that doesn't make sense to me. The Wheel of Thought, I know, must have access to the Valynan weapons. They could easily paralyze or kill us with their special orb weaponry. I imagine that orb we saw has such an ability."

"So they must only be monitoring us."

"Yes, I would imagine so."

"But why?"

"There could be several reasons. Perhaps the Wheel of Thought just wants to watch us at the moment and see what our plans are. Or perhaps they want to make sure we don't speak out about the Order. If we do, we may have to escape or outwit that orb we saw."

Ranum stirred on the metal bench that ran perpendicular to the one where Naria had just been sleeping. He groaned as he sat up, and yawned, the morning light filling the cavity of his mouth. Nadan turned to look at him.

"It is your turn to steer," he said.

Ranum made his way slowly to the front cockpit, while Nadan moved off to the side to allow him in. It was at that moment that Nadan caught sight of something glinting off in the western horizon.

He took out his telescoping glasses from his robe and adjusted the lens for long range. The objects he saw were still small and indistinct through the heat waves and blowing sand, but he recognized the familiar architectural outlines and shapes immediately. He had seen those multi-colored, extravagantly patterned domes so many times in books he had read in Simkada. His heart was racing. For a moment, he relived in his mind the imagery of his dreams of Kira Mandi: the dark faces, the red sand gusting in the streets, and the tall, writhing, exotic towers.

"What do you see?" said Naria. She seemed to sense the sudden intensity of his feeling.

"Kira Mandi," he said. His voice was tremulous with excitement.

"I see you have thought long and deeply about this place," she said.

Nadan took off his telescoping glasses and looked at her. Her thoughts were piercing him like the desert Light Star over their heads the day before. Her red hair was shimmering crimson-gold in that light now, tresses blown back along her face.

"I have seen this place many times in my dreams before I embarked on this journey," he said. "I haven't been able to interpret them. But I have an indescribable attraction to this place, almost as if I have been here many times."

"I knew a dream interpreter at the Order," Naria said. "His name was Orona. I imagine he could tell the meaning of it."

"Well, I'm not sure I will need an interpretation," said Nadan. "The uriel said my questions will be answered when I enter the city."

Ranum, who had been scanning the horizon with his own telescoping glasses, suddenly folded the glasses up and put them back into his breast pocket. "If the city is close, shouldn't we change our clothes?" asked Ranum. "I do not think we want to look like Valynans entering the city. It might be dangerous."

It was true. Ranum was wearing a red garment, embroidered with bold, charcoal Valynan letters on each side. Nadan was wearing a green robe, sprinkled with shapes of a silver fish. The fish was an emblem of Valynan aristocracy.

Ranum glanced at Nadan's robe for a second. "I do not think you can change their attitudes in this way, as you tried in Valyna," he remarked, critically.

"That is not my only reason," said Nadan. "If we travel as Mandians, we would raise suspicion. They would see through it immediately and see it as deceitful."

"Then we should travel as Simkadans," said Ranum.

"You can do as you like," said Nadan.

Nadan took over driving the skiff, while Ranum retreated to the rear of the vehicle to change his clothes. They were getting closer to the city, and they could all see the towers now without the aid of telescoping glasses. Dark clouds were shaping and molding themselves furiously over the southern rim of the city, creating a blackened backdrop against the glistening towers. The sand around the city was dark red, almost crimson. It was a color of the desert they hadn't encountered yet in their journey, and, together with the somber clouds overhead, it gave the desert atmosphere a fiery, mystical depth.

They were soon at the gates of the city, two giant red half circles in the sand, dividing two different skiff lanes that coursed in and out of the city. As they got closer, they saw no traffic was moving out of the city. When they were at the edge of the gates, a white beam of light shot from the side of the gate, blocking them from entering. Ranum tried to maneuver the skiff through it, but he found the vehicle immobilized in the air. He tried to reverse the skiff, but it wouldn't move backward either.

The air hummed with a strange twining sound from the laser beam, as a hooded man wearing orange pants and a red shirt appeared at the side of the gate and walked toward them. Even as he saw the man, Nadan began rolling a mind-influencing meta phrase through his mind.

When the man reached them, he pulled off what looked like a layer of skin from his face. Nadan realized it was a special mask, probably used to block the sand and the wind while he was at his post.

"The city is closed to outlanders at the moment," said the man. The man spoke the common tongue with a fiery, transcendent air.

"We are from Simkada," said Ranum.

Nadan could sense his friend now saying the meta as well. The man frowned deeply and looked out across the desert, the red glow illuminating his features so that he almost appeared to be blushing. Nadan could sense, however, the man was still as a stone inside but distrustful.

"I see you are a Simkadan, which is fine," said the man, disinterestedly. "But your friend here is wearing Valynan garb."

"I'm a Valynan, but I am also a Simkadan," said Nadan. "But when I walk into your city, I will become a Mandian."

All the energy of the gathering meta was now flowing into the man's mind, like a river into the desert. The man's face was still slightly doubtful, but the edges of his face seemed warmer now than the crimson glow on the desert. The man let out a short laugh. "Your friend here been drinking too much clinus?" he said to Ranum.

The words were barely out of the man's mouth before he fell over on the sand. The light beam transfixed on their vehicle suddenly evaporated, and Ranum gunned the craft forward into the city.

"What did you do that for?" asked Nadan. He knew immediately Ranum had done another one of his paralysis metas on the man.

"Vanik," Ranum said, saying the Simkadan swear. "I didn't like the way he was talking to you. I probed his mind, too, and I perceived that he had no intention of letting us in, even with your meta."

"You shouldn't have done that so hastily," said Nadan. "It's better to use diplomacy first. We might have to be on our guards now, as renegades in this city. The meta would have worked in a few minutes."

"Well, you shouldn't be saying things like that to guards at the city," said Ranum, slightly angry but not daring to really challenge Nadan like he did other people. He was known for his blustery temper in Simkada. "I know what you are doing, but it's not helping us appear normal."

They found themselves at an intersection of four stone roads which all converged at this one place before the gates. Merchants and nomads scurried about in the shadowy sunlight beneath small, slanted tents. Over them were three domed towers, painted with strange beasts and writing on their sides, spaced in between each of the roads. Nadan blanketed a series of metas across the city, which evoked friendliness. He also did a memory-blocking meta on the guard at the city's gates about the whole incident, a trick Naria had taught him back in Valyna.

"Well, we're here, finally," said Naria. "Those metas were so strong, we probably won't have much to worry about."

Nadan said nothing. He was staring, enchanted by the haunting towers and gilded domes all about, ones he had seen so often in his dreams. Nadan had never felt something so ancient. He felt the architecture was but an outer manifestation for a deeper energy that permeated this place. He sensed ancient but playful reverence underpinning life in Kira Mandi. He sensed lives stretching back endlessly into the dawn of civilization, back millions of years. He had never sensed such oldness in a culture or a place.

"Which road should we take?" asked Ranum.

"I think we should take the middle one," said Naria.

"Nadan?" Ranum asked.

For a moment, Nadan took his mind off the soul of the city.

"Yes, the middle one seems good to me also," he said.

Ranum moved slowly through the crowd of nomads and merchants, then started to speed up the craft after they were on the thoroughfare. However, the street itself was almost as jammed with people as the intersection was, and he had to slow the craft down again. Nomads with dark faces and turbans, and women with baskets on their heads, hemmed them in on all sides, chattering in some unfamiliar Mandian dialect.

They had been traveling only a few minutes when the storm hit them, sweeping sheets of rain across the crowds. For a few minutes, there was chaos, as the crowds started moving quickly down the street. Ranum had to stop the skiff almost completely. But then everyone vanished, and the street became almost completely vacant, except for a few beggars in corners of kaaraadruun huts, angling their faces up at the warm rain, filling their mouths with the water. The storm was now intensifying; lightning crashed over their heads. Water fell in torrents. Nadan and Naria quickly put up the canopy on the skiff, and they moved along the street again, the rain thrumming on the metal roof over their heads.

"I read about this place in Valyna," said Ranum.

He slowed the skiff. Nadan looked out through the small glass portal by his seat. He saw a small kaaraadruun apartment, painted white with angled black stripes running down the side. Two flags—one red, the other blue—flipped around in the storm gusts, on metal poles protruding from the second story of the building. On a creaking wooden sign over the rusted metal doorway of the hut, a sign read "The Faquin."

"It's an inn," said Ranum. "We can stay here tonight."

They waited inside the skiff for another half hour for the storm to pass. Then they all got out of the vehicle. Ranum went inside and paid for the sleeping chambers while Nadan and Naria both carried their belongings to their rooms, which were up on the highest floor overlooking the city.

Upstairs, they found three small rooms, all connected together by a single hallway and living area. Nadan's room was a pentagonal chamber with a low ceiling and faced in a southerly direction. Doors opened from the chamber onto a small patio on top of the roof, with a small stone chair and a circular fountain tinkling gently in the air. Nadan threw open the doors and stepped out on it, inhaling the rain-scented air. He had been so preoccupied with the storm and the other activities that he had forgotten to focus so intently on the soul, the collective will, of the city. But there it was now, that same realm of being that had haunted his dreams back in Simkada. The view of the desert area was most similar to where they had met the Anatami, but this place was like a cocoon, a sanctuary from the vanities and struggles he had been facing. Like the desert, the scene conveyed an empty loveliness, whose ancientness seemed to extend out into the void it so closely bordered. His thoughts strayed out into that void. His eyes couldn't see much of the Great Fault, the Gortag, from where he was standing, but he could see the horizon line fall off into an infinite reddish blue in the distance, where the land plummeted into universal space.

For a moment, he felt a rumbling beneath his feet, similar to what he had felt the day he had left Simkada. Was it the ajnir awareness shaking him, or was it the collective will of the city, quaking with the emotional disturbance of the future? His mind stumbled in uncertainty for a moment. There was much pain in this city, in addition to the feeling of isolated peace. It was at that moment that he sensed catastrophe lurking here, as if waves of the future would someday consume it. He could sense the remnants of war here and the fragile treaty that kept it at bay. But he felt a new energy, a new hope, moving in from across the void, like a gentle wave, and then, all of it diving ever more deeply into violence and bloodshed.

"The air is sweet," said a soft voice by him.

It was Naria next to him. Her red hair was flowing backward, like a river. How long had she been standing next to him?

"Your mind is wandering far outside its ordinary borders," said Naria. "But I cannot sense all that you are perceiving."

"I was thinking of this entire city, and what it has been and what it will be," Nadan said.

"What has it been?" she asked.

"It has been a world apart from the rest, a place forgotten and downtrodden," he said.

"And what will it become?"

"That is what I keep asking myself. I feel as if a great amount of good will come to this city. But when it does, it will bring with it an equal amount of tragedy. Beyond that I cannot see."

"Klohar, the ancient ajnir seer, once said blessings and tragedy are inseparable," said Naria.

"I suppose he was right," said Nadan. "But what do you feel here, yourself?"

Naria paused for a moment. Out over the desert, thunder rumbled and cracked, splitting open the moist silence lingering over the urban landscape.

"I feel a mixture of things," she said. "I do not sense the greed or the rushing or the haste of my culture. I feel this place is somehow deeply in touch with Dinjin, more so than any other place I have ever been, except perhaps for that area we visited near the Anatami. I wonder if there are many ajnir in this city."

Nadan hadn't thought of this. He knew there must be other ajnir in this city, but he could not sense where they were. Would they have formed an order like the one in Valyna? For a moment, he scanned his mind for everything Manalk had told him before he departed. The ajnir had rarely spoken of his childhood days in Kira Mandi. He never had said who had discovered him or what the ajnir of this city were like. Nadan spread his mind out into the moist air, seeking for any sign of them, but he heard no immediate response to his inner call, just the abbreviated, knife-like cry of a carrion bird over his head.

Naria had now moved to the edge of the balcony they were on and was twisting her hair into a small braid.

"I sense something else, too," she said. "Although this place is in deeper connection with Dinjin, I also sense something is not right with it. There are ways in which Valyna may be better than this place."

"In what way?" asked Nadan, drawing closer to her on the balcony.

She paused. The curtains inside the door were stirring. The silence over the desert was interrupted by the sound of a horn off in the distance. Nadan slid his arm around Naria's shoulders. The next instant, they were kissing.

"Dinner is ready," called Ranum from inside.

"We will be in shortly," said Nadan. He stood at the edge of the balcony, holding the girl in his arms.

"I am told we have a visitor down below, waiting for us," said Ranum, coming out on the balcony.

Nadan was startled. "We've only just arrived," he said. "How could anyone know we are here?"

Ranum didn't answer, but he seemed worried. Nadan wondered if his strange call just moments before had perhaps had its desired effect. But this was odd. He would most likely have recognized any response to his inward voice. He turned, and Naria followed him from the balcony into the lower chambers. Ranum came last, letting a red towel drag at his feet behind him.

Beyond the city, to the east, the thunderstorm rumbled, then disappeared into a gray mist hanging out over the desert.

Chapter 14

The Great Fault

A servant led them along the circuitous corridors of the kaaraadruun hut, dimly lit on each
side by small lumin-globes set inside the mud-caked
walls. The corridors twisted through the lair, like a
serpent, and moved steadily downward at an angle.
Eventually, the corridor fell down some steps, leading through a small archway and into a hallway filled
with graffiti-like mythological figures painted onto
darkly painted walls.

Nadan recognized some of the images: Askal, the
mythological warrior who battled the sun lord Dul-
man and vanquished him; Thorag, the wise leader of
the city in the pre-futuristic era who was said to have
lived 750 years; and Dilao, the famous epic writer of
Kira Mandi.

As he looked at the pictures, a shadow stirred in
the far corner of the hall. Nadan realized it wasn't a
shadow at all but a man standing there, so still that
his black robe seemed part of the shaded wall. The
man came over and stood, facing them. He was tall
and large-framed and loomed a bit menacingly above
them; his face breathed intelligence. On his left cheek,

he bore a large crescent-shaped scar. On his ears, two large silver earrings glinted in the dim light.

"I saw you come in the city today, near the gates," he said. "We don't have many Simkadans here. I know who you are."

"Are you from the Wheel of Thought?" asked Nadan, blanching a little bit. The way the man said "I know who you are" made him feel suddenly uneasy.

"No, I have no affiliations with the world of Valyna, much like my other Mandians," he said. "I am Korbluun. Toruna, your friend, sent me a letter in the last few months, telling me that you would be here eventually. It wasn't too hard to spot you. We don't have many outlanders visit here at the moment."

The man smiled a little, but his face was sort of gaunt, placid, mostly serious. He pulled a small brown wooden pipe from his pocket, took an inhale, and then exhaled the smoke slowly toward the octagonal western-facing window of the inn. The scent of resinous tobacco, mixed with Kurieme, filled the air.

Might still be the Order, said Ranum to Nadan, telepathically. *They know who Toruna is.* Nadan glanced at his friend, but his face remained unflinching. He still wasn't sure. Though he thought it odd Korbluun had found him, Nadan sensed no dishonesty in the man's presence. Yet, he could not detect the man was telepathic, which would have been a clear indication of him being an ajnir.

"How did you find us here?" he asked finally, cooly.

"The Fanquin is the closest inn to the city's gates," replied Korbluun, casually, taking a seat on the bench near the wall. "Travelers almost always end up here on their first night in the city. Not too hard to figure out. Toruna said you wanted to see the Gortag, is that right?"

Ranum didn't say anything, but the suspicion was still apparent in his expression. Nadan looked at him with greater interest.

"That's why we came here," he said.

"Some prefer to see it during the day, but I prefer it at night," Korbluun said. "One can see more deeply into the night sky, and I happen to be an astronomer. I think you would enjoy the view more at night. You can join me if you like tonight."

Nadan felt puzzled. He sensed Korbluun was not telepathic, and yet there was an awareness to his presence that suggested some profound insight. He wondered if the man was an ajnir who had not yet awakened to this fact.

Nadan conferred silently with his friends: *I sense this man means us no harm.* Sensing the same, Naria gave her nonverbal agreement, almost instantly. Ranum was slightly more reluctant, but his inward voice finally bubbled into Nadan's mind after a few seconds: *I will go if you like.*

Korbluun was sitting in the shadows, stirring the ashes in his pipe and packing it with Kurieme and tobacco.

"I sense you are distrustful of me," said Korbluun, standing up after placing the pipe in his pocket. "You must have enemies somewhere. Do I guess wrong? It's a pity, the world the way it is. All three cities are now at war in one way or another, and not one of the cities' peoples trusts another. You have nothing to worry from me. I have no hatred of Simkadans."

"Some Valynans have been tracking us here and there," asked Nadan. "I don't want to say much more about that."

"You can meet me at the main path that leads from the edge of the city," Korbluun replied. "All you must do is follow this thoroughfare until the end. The sign in front of the path reads Jakelpiodies."

"The Broken Road," translated Nadan beneath his breath.

"I see you know our language," Korbluun said.

"I knew a Mandian man in my native land," said Nadan. "He taught me some of it."

"That's as strange as it is to see you here."

"Will you join us for our meal?" said Nadan, pointing to the low tables along the wall.

"Of course," said Korbluun.

After dinner, Korbluun, Nadan, Naria, and Ranum tramped outside the inn and into the streets, weaving among the beggars lined up in chaotic rows all the way down the thoroughfare, which wound like a snaking, dark river into the night. It was something none of them had really confronted before in the cities of their birth: a massive, sprawling, endless poverty that seemed to stretch all around them, choking their minds, withering their souls. As he walked, Nadan's mind moved out among them, feeling the lifeless apathy and despair that moved like some dark, malevolent phantasm among these unprivileged masses. He wondered at the incongruity of the city: while it seemed to intersect more deeply with Dinjin, it was somehow more removed from its benefits.

"I was wondering the same thing," said Naria, sensing his thought.

"But why is that?" asked Nadan. "Does the Dinjin create disease and poverty?"

"I do not think so," said Naria. "I think the people of this city have been so concentrated on Dinjin that they have forgotten this world, in some sense. In Valyna, it is the opposite."

This appeased Nadan's mind some, but he still felt confused. Dinjin was supposed to be a place where good dreams manifested easily, Manalk had said, where food and sustenance were abundant at the mere willing.

The road they were walking on suddenly narrowed, and the connected kaaraadruun huts disappeared alongside them. There were no beggars in this stretch of the highway, and the travelers were confronted by a deep sense of vacancy and stillness. A barren wasteland surrounded them, littered with small cacti and low shrubs. Small huts were sprinkled across the low plain. Nadan sensed the ominous sense of space off in the darkness just beyond them, in the west. He could feel the Great Fault there, waiting like some opening into another realm, an abyss of almost frightening infinity. They walked for a few more minutes, until they finally saw a large sign with lumin-globes on its upper corners, illuminating the phrase: Jakelpiodies.

Korbluun moved out from the edge of the sign and held up a large oblong metal case in his left hand that he had been holding the whole time while walking with them.

"I brought my tripod and telescope," he said. "You shall behold stars you have never seen before tonight. The eastern horizon line where you have lived does not show stars that revolve below Urshan Dai."

"I had heard of those constellations," said Nadan. "Geropata, I remember, is one, though I have never studied astronomy to any great extent."

"If the clouds over the Fault are not deep, we might see Geropata, or the Iron Dragon, as they call it in Mandi," said Korbluun. "It is distant and therefore difficult to see at times. There are also the radiations over the Fault, which distort visual perception."

"Radiations?" said Nadan.

"Strange radiations have been forming over the Fault for the last few years. We astronomers have been studying the phenomenon. As you look out across the Fault into deep space, you may sometimes notice coloration shifts in the atmosphere. These are the radiations. None of our scientists can yet explain them."

Korbluun turned and led them through a small opening in the scraggly desert scrubs bordering the sign. Nadan went first, and Naria and Ranum came after him, warily watching the sides around and behind them. The path moved in a straight line toward the Fault, then dipped into a small gully in the sandy floor at their feet. It moved through an area filled with large rocks, then turned and zig-zagged through the wandering graveyard of haunting stones. Graffiti covered the stones, primitive shapes in black or fluorescent colors. The words beneath the figures were written in Mandian, and Nadan couldn't decipher them. The rocky area suddenly tapered off, and they found themselves in a flatter, even more desolate landscape, the lifeless ribbon of barren desert surrounding the Great Fault. Nadan suddenly sensed that Ranum's mind, watchful and distrustful, had attuned him to some other awareness behind them in the dark.

Do you think we are being followed? Ranum telepathed to him.

Nadan stretched his mind into the black void behind them. All he could sense was wind and dust, a few lizards scratching the stones and licking their bodies, a mouse preening its hairs with its paws. Then, he sensed it: some malevolent, indifferent consciousness swirling in their wake, among the stones, exhaling and inhaling roughly. The being suddenly became aware of Nadan's telepathing and faded into the distance, wrapping itself as if into some other dimension where Nadan couldn't perceive its hidden psychology.

It felt like that strange, black telepath orb we saw back in Valyna, Nadan returned finally to Ranum.

He didn't have much time to ponder this issue further because suddenly the ridge before him dropped down at his feet, and his heart fluttered at the sight before him. The Great Fault was not as sheer in this place as it had been depicted in paintings back in Simkada. The earth angled down beneath his feet at a steep but not entirely vertical angle. Beyond it was a sense of dizzying, eternal spaciousness. It was as if Nadan had seen the image a thousand times in his dreams. The pale stars clung in the sky, each burning, like tiny brilliant sunrises out of some distant world. Nadan stretched his mind into the void beyond the precipice; a sensation of exiting terrestrial gravitation overwhelmed him. He was lost in a sea of ambient spatial awareness that was both liberating and terrifying.

But as he looked at the scene, he realized the breathtaking imagery of the place was but a disguise, a cloak, for a deeper reality that surged through this place. He sensed the Dinjin, moving through it, as though it were unseen, electric wind.

Naria and Ranum both seemed to sense it as well.

"The Dinjin is stronger here than anywhere else I have been," said Ranum.

As soon as the words were out of his mouth, Nadan returned to his normal state of mind. He and Naria both looked at Ranum. As soon as they did, Ranum realized what he had done.

Korbluun was just ahead of them and had obviously heard the word "Dinjin" from his mouth. He turned and looked at them with the same enigmatic expression Nadan had seen back at the Jakelpiodies sign.

"I see you are guntaras," he said.

"What are guntaras?" asked Nadan.

"That is what they are called in Mandi, but the ancient word is ajnir," said Korbluun.

A ball of densely rolled-up straw and papers blew across the barren wasteland behind Korbluun and down the sheer slope, into the Fault.

"I did not sense you were an ajnir before," said Nadan.

"We are not deceptive, but we don't believe in ostentation," said Korbluun.

"But didn't you perceive our thoughts when we were telepathing?" asked Nadan.

"I have no reason to use that power."

"And do the ajnir here never use their psychic abilities?"

"Rarely. I myself do not even have the ability. I have never trained myself to use it."

Korbluun took his pipe from his cloak, lit it with a match, then inhaled from it. The wind swept the smoke away in a quick movement.

"And what do you train yourself in?" asked Nadan.

He was now feeling a little suspicious, like Ranum. He wondered: *Could Korbluun be pretending to be an ajnir in the Order to obtain more of the ancient secrets?* He shared the thought for a moment with Ranum, who expressed his tacit agreement.

Korbluun smiled. Nadan had seen the same cool, unperturbed look before on Manalk's face. The expression was like a piece of silent space in the middle of a universe, completely still, while everything around it swirled in a restless maelstrom. Nadan felt magnetized to it, like the first time he had met Manalk. The expression on Korbluun's face dissipated.

"I see now," said Nadan, humbly, his eyes trailing off into the space beyond the Gortag.

Korbluun inhaled from the pipe, turned, and walked to the edge of the slope, which ran down into the Fault, then placed his metal case on the ground. He unwound some ropes strung around the case, then snapped the object open. Still feeling his subtle, disguised power, Nadan moved over to his side, as Korbluun pulled out his instruments and began stringing them together into a small tripod. Ranum and Naria both came after him, watching the landscape over the Fault.

Korbluun had just begun adjusting the lens of the telescope, which was now mounted on the tripod, when Naria spoke.

"Look," she said.

She was pointing her finger at the black void. Nadan looked up and saw immediately what had startled her: a bluish-crimson ribbon of energy wavering across the atmosphere over the Fault. It rippled and billowed like a cloud of smoke in a slight breeze for a moment, then vanished completely.

"Those must be the radiations," said Nadan.

"Yes," said Korbluun. "They happen often in this area for some reason."

Korbluun drew his gaze from the telescope and looked at her sharply.

"We guntaras have often looked at them and wondered," he said. "The Dinjin is strong in this place. It has been that way for eons. We have wondered if perhaps the radiations are from Dinjin or another realm like it, of which we are totally unaware. Our scientists, however, believe the lights are just electrical disturbances over the Fault. "

Korbluun pivoted the telescope, so Nadan could see into it.

"There is Geropata," Korbluun said.

Nadan, looking through the small eyeglass, gazed at the intricate configuration of stars he had only seen in books before and was never able to see at night from Simkada. The constellation looked like a small head of a beast, with a slithering chain of stars trailing out behind it. Iron Dragon. He had never heard the term Korbluun had used, but it was aptly named. The bluish, chilly hued band of stars must have reminded the ancient Mandians of the sheen of iron and was roughly formed into the shape of a twirling serpent or dragon.

Nadan stepped aside, so Ranum and Naria could peer into it.

"Tell me, Korbluun," he said. "Have you studied much about where the other half of our planet has gone?"

"Most scientists of our day believe the other half of the planet split off 40,000 years ago and was swallowed up by our Light Star, Urum. A minority believes the seismic activity that caused the split jettisoned the other half of the planet, known as Eroma, out of our solar system altogether. Still another group believes the other half orbited around the planet for a while, before being dismembered by meteors."

Korbluun paused.

"And what do you think?" Nadan asked.

"Well, I do not have a clear-cut theory at this point, but I am disappointed with both beliefs," said Korbluun. "If either were to be true, our planet would have been rocked out of its orbit completely. Yet my calculations show that our orbit has not changed for eons."

He inhaled from his pipe again and let the smoke trail slowly out from his nostrils, as he stared into the landscape of stars.

"But then where could the other half of the planet have gone?" asked Naria.

"We don't know for certain, nor do we have another theory," said Korbluun. "Some believe Eroma just vaporized completely. Some guntaras believe it went into one of the alternative universes. But none can explain how such a thing would happen or, if it did, why all Urshan Dai wasn't warped into it as well."

There was silence for a moment, soon interrupted by the hissing of something like a snake or lizard behind them. Nadan, however, was completely oblivious to the sound, so intent was he on the subject at hand.

"That seems right to me," Nadan said after a pause. "If Eroma was in this universe, we ajnir would know of it. But I suppose if the sun had swallowed it up, we might not know of it. Are there any records in Valyna of that time period?"

"There are some," said Korbluun. "What we can tell from them is limited. There were earthquakes during that time period, a fact that has given credence to the belief that seismic activity caused the fracture. But it seems to have happened all of a sudden. People woke up one day, and the other half of the planet was gone. It was a terrible event, but it didn't seem to take many lives in Kira Mandi for some reason."

A story Nadan had read over and over in Simkada returned to his mind. It told of a man named Galandrim, who had traveled across the city for a day. When he had returned, he had found the other half of the planet gone, and with it, his entire family and all of his possessions. He had written a poem about the tragedy. Scholars quibbled about the authenticity of its origins, but one phrase of the poem was still etched in Nadan's memory:

That planet is a dream; ice world
That knows no fiction of dawn:
Mother, wife, child—through space exhumed—
Their space within this space, now utterly gone:
Deathless love, bitterly consumed.

"I wonder if other civilizations are still existing today, somewhere on Eroma," Ranum mused, as if in another world.

"It's unlikely, especially if that world is still here in our universe," said Korbluun. "If they flew out of our solar system, they would have soon been frozen."

At that moment, they saw another flash of bluish-gold radiance over the Fault, a shimmering wave that moved and swilled in the atmosphere, then vaporized. This one was closer than they had seen before. Nadan got a better sense of the phenomenon this time. It didn't feel like a normal electrical current. It seemed to him more like what Naria often described as a wave of mental electricity. He was having a strange feeling, as if he had seen this sight many times before. "Flashes from Dinjin," Nadan murmured.

"Mmmm," said Korbluun, next to him, catching his soft intonation. "So we believe."

He walked over to the telescope and began taking it apart, placing the separate pieces carefully into the case he had been carrying.

"Have you ever seen apparitions here?" Nadan suddenly asked. "We call them uriels in the west."

Out of the corner of his eye, Nadan saw Naria catch her breath and look downward.

"I have not seen such things as you speak about, but I have heard of them," he said. "Some guntaras here have communicated with them. I know little about them. There is another ajnir named Cropaayaa. I know he has spoken with them and has studied the phenomenon. You can visit him tomorrow, if you like."

"We would appreciate that, Korbluun," said Nadan. "One has spoken to me already. I would like to know more."

Korbluun looked at him with a piercing glance. Nadan could tell he was slightly suspicious of the uriel phenomenon. But the Mandian quickly looked away, then picked up his telescope and tripod.

They moved back down the path again toward the city. The Kindri moon was now directly over their heads, banishing the shadows that had loomed at the backs of the graffiti stones. Nadan searched around with his mind again for the strange black creature they had sensed earlier, but it was gone. The air in the barren land felt ascetic and serene, with no tinge of malevolence.

They wound along the desert path for a short distance, until they arrived at the Jakelpiodies sign again. Korbluun went with them for a short while along the main thoroughfare, until they came to the crowded inner city streets again, with kaaraadruun huts stacked deeply on each side. After telling them where Cropaayaa's hut was, Korbluun disappeared for the night into a dark street that intersected the thoroughfare. Naria, Ranum, and Nadan kept walking along the thoroughfare, back to the inn.

When they finally reached their quarters, Nadan lay down on his cot and quickly fell into a dreamless sleep. He was awakened hours later by a terrible, oppressive feeling. As he lay there in the darkness, his scalp tingled. At first he thought it was the uriel, but then he realized it was much different. Even as he had the thought, he saw the creature itself. It was black, a shimmering image that pulsated and blinked in and out of his eyesight. Like a uriel, its face was featureless, but Nadan sensed a powerful gravitational force surrounding it, pulling all emotions and thoughts into itself. The peaceful atmosphere in his room seemed to wither and retreat in the air.

The being moved toward him slowly, creeping over the settee near his bed. Nadan pulled the blankets up around him, hoping to ward it away. But it was a useless gesture. The being extended a transparent, trembling hand, thrusting it through the blanket and into his heart, pulling his life energy into itself with strange magnetic strength. Panic swept over him. He had experienced the other world it was trying to bring him to before. The being felt like the personal embodiment of that terrible world. All that realm's rage, darkness, despondency, and violence were contained within this dark form, it seemed, in a single point of awareness.

Why do you resist the inevitable? the being telepathed to him.

Its mental voice was scathing and grating, tearing through his psychology. It halted its struggle for a moment, staring at him. The air around its face swirled and glimmered with a grimacing air.

What is inevitable? Nadan returned.

This is what you must do to rejoin your master, it said.

Why do you want me to go to Mazag? Nadan said. *I sense you have another motive than just to bring me to the feet of Manalk.*

The being seemed to laugh, shivering coldly. Then it spat some black, liquid-like electricity into the air. Then, it seemed to almost begin choking, pulling liquid or energy from its mouth with its strange invisible hands. It crouched on the corner of his bed for almost a minute, on a red cushion near his feet, pulling energy from its mouth and spitting it into the room. A dark feeling of depression and anxiety began to fill Nadan's mind. For a moment, Nadan almost felt a certain pity for it. The creature stopped spitting energy from its mouth, stared at him for a moment, then leaned over and began pulling at Nadan's feet, his inner form. It soon resumed its struggle with his life force, pulling and grabbing at him with increased intensity. As it pulled and pulled, Nadan felt his mind beginning to yield to its uncanny gravitational force. The room around him became cloudy, hazy. He became aware of a large, black, invisible ocean over his head. As his mind moved through this expanse, he began to dimly become aware of the Mazag above him, its energy, as if waiting for him, calling him.

As he thought his awareness was just about to slip into it, a bluish light suddenly filled the room. It came from beneath his bed and gently touched him on the forehead. It was a uriel, perhaps the same one he had seen in Simkada. It turned toward the black shape and began pulling it gently, thread by thread, off his body. Soon, all the black fibers were gone, and Nadan felt the malevolent being dissolve and disappear into the night. The evening was peaceful again in the air, and serenity returned like a flower in spring. He was left with the uriel crouching on top of his body. It was in the form of a spider-like being, with seven or so legs protruding from a central core of its form.

Nadan bowed his head before it.

You have saved me, he said.

The creature pivoted its head toward his window, pierced with moonlight, but said nothing. Each of its spindly legs went up into itself, until it was in a roughly shaped humanoid figure again, with four rough-hewn, blurry limbs. Nadan sensed it was about to leave.

Please tell me more of my mission, Nadan asked quickly. *What am I doing in Kira Mandi?*

The creature floated up into the air, saying nothing in response. It seemed to be weighing many thoughts all at once with an intense clarity. It remained silent, hovering, almost bobbing in the air. Then it shimmered, faded, and moved slowly off across the room, vanishing into the wall and into the night.

Chapter 15

Cropaayaa

When he awoke, Nadan decided not to tell Ranum and Naria of his experience with the dark being the night before. Something told him that he shouldn't say anything. He understood that telling others about the experience might open them to the energy of the Mazag creature as well. It was the way of the Hidden Realms, Manalk had told him. The more one contemplated and entertained thoughts, negative or positive, the more they infiltrated one's being.

Nadan got up and splashed water on his face, then threw his robe on. At that same moment, Naria came in his chamber, wearing a bright yellow robe and a red sari over her head, the same garb the Mandian women were accustomed to wearing.

"Korbluun already stopped by the inn earlier," she said. "He said he can't make it this morning, but he left directions to Cropaayaa's abode."

She handed him a small yellow piece of parchment, with directions from The Faquin to the ajnir's hut. Korbluun wrote "Blessings from Sahala" at the bottom of the note.

"What's Sahala?" asked Nadan.

"I already asked someone on the street," said Naria. "They didn't know, but I believe that word means Dinjin in Mandian."

The time was only 24 gyras. They ate breakfast at the inn, which featured a strange reddish sour fruit called uipel that they had never tasted before.

"This place feels like home," said Nadan, after a while.

"It's like you have been here before," said Naria, mysteriously. She was sitting in the corner of the downstairs chamber of the inn, staring out the windows at a flock of gorlon birds pecking at the street. Nadan was beginning to get used to her perceptive ability and had grown to appreciate it. Her thoughts were like a subtle guide to him.

"I *have* been here before, in my dreams," said Nadan.

"I've read those before in you," said Naria. "But I sense it is more than that. I'm not sure what."

They ate the rest of their meal in silence. When they had finished, the servants came and cleared their dishes and eating utensils. Ranum went upstairs to change his clothes. Then they went outside, where they found the street bustling with its usual commotion.

Ranum led them through the streets, pausing at every turn to check the signs on the streets to avoid getting lost. The old women, dressed in their red and blue and yellow saris, carrying baskets of bread through the streets, watched them curiously as they went, especially Ranum. His gold hair, shining fiercely in the sunlight, was a rare sight in Kira Mandi.

They kept weaving through the dense crowds for a while, until they came to a quieter alleyway in the southern end of the city. The kaaraadruun huts were noticeably larger and more expensive in this section of the city. Many had three or four stories, with terraces full of fronds and delicate white flowers, angling up and down layered steps. They would have seemed shoddy in comparison to the great sprawling mansions Nadan saw in Valyna. But, nonetheless, they were visibly more stately than the one- and two-story, simple kaaraadruun huts they had been walking through just minutes ago.

"This must be the Ralisk, the wealthy section in Kira Mandi," said Nadan.

They kept walking, until Ranum finally halted abruptly outside one of the few smaller, undistinguished huts along the thoroughfare. The hut they were in front of was wedged between two large four-story huts that shot upward in the sky; their gilded domes seemed to melt almost into the radiance of Light Star over their heads. In the lee of both structures, the shade appeared cool, an oasis of shadow in the blaring heat. Two green fronds were stationed on each side of the small portal doorway. Hanging from the doorpost were some small metallic green and red chimes, clinking slightly in the faint breeze. "I know your names already," said a man appearing inside the door. "Korbluun told me about your journey to the Great Fault last night. What was your first reaction?"

As he moved out into the sunlight, Nadan could see Cropaayaa was a short, bald man, with wide warrior-like hairy shoulders and a straightforward, masculine expression. His face was darker than most Mandians, almost jet black. One long silver earring stretched from his left lobe to his bare shoulder. A gold bracelet circled his right arm.

"Well, I felt some fear initially, then a sense of expansion, almost liberation," said Nadan.

The man moved out of the shadows of the hut, rubbing his chin with his palm. He stared up at the roof for a second. "Fear, then expansion," he mused. "That is better you felt that way. If you had felt the reverse, I would have been more concerned."

"You are concerned about my emotions?"

"Well, yes, first reactions and impulses to things are sometimes namiz. Did you not know?"

"To an extent, not so much. My teacher, Manalk, told me it was some unusual event, such as a mood change in people. Things of that sort."

"Mmmm, yes," said Cropaayaa, rubbing his chin again. "Those work too. But the Gortag is special, I tell you. Just sitting there for a while will tell you things about yourself in general. But the first reaction to Gortag is always the most important for a person. It shows a person where his life is going. If you had felt the fear second, that would have indicated you were not ready to be free of your mental constraints in this lifetime. If you feel some fear first, then freedom, it means you are ready to let go of what you shouldn't become in this life. At least, that is what my teacher, Sanga, always told me. But come: we can talk inside about the reason for your visit. Korbluun spoke of your interest to me already."

They all walked inside the man's shadowy hut, where their eyes met a long table littered with tin and brass cups. A small pot was rattling on top of a small heat-globe in the corner of the room. Cropaayaa offered them all drinks of a Mandian spice drink, kaliy, which they sipped on stools at the edge of the table.

"Have you studied namiz much?" the man asked Nadan, after they were all sitting.

"Not too much. Manalk saw namiz here, he told me." He told the man how Manalk had first told him about the namiz of people falling suddenly silent in a crowd, years ago when he had been in Kira Mandi. Manalk interpreted this as a namiz that there was some profound change in the society of the planet.

"Ah, those hushes on people," said Cropaayaa, his voice lowering. "We've been seeing those here and there in the city. Not sure what they mean, personally. Korbluun said you wanted to learn more about the uriel."

"Yes," said Nadan, distractedly.

Cropaayaa went over and turned off the heat-globe, with his smooth, calm, brown hands, and the cups and pans slowly stopped rattling. Then, he walked over to the edge of the room and pressed his palm against the wall. The wall heaved. A thin, almost imperceptible fissure appeared along the surface of the wall, which slowly folded inward. A gust of cool air blew up from the tunneled staircase, leading below.

"Down here, you will find an ancient, secret chamber of the guntaras," he said. "I am its caretaker. We have a few writings on the uriel. Not too many."

Cropaayaa pulled a pen-like handheld lumin-globe from his pocket, flicking a switch on it. The room and the shadows in the staircase leading below stole away before its green radiance. Ranum, Naria, and then Nadan followed him below down the wet stone staircase, which spiraled downward into the darkness. As they neared the bottom of the stair-case, Nadan felt a draft blowing across his knees and bare feet, a sign they were entering a larger space or cavern. Even as he reached the bottom of the stair-case, Cropaayaa's lumin-globe went out, and they were suddenly immersed in sheer blackness. Sounds of scuffling resounded around the echoing cavern, as Cropaayaa fidgeted for a lumin-globe in the dark-ness. Then, a small light sprouted in one corner of the room, a faint reddish glow. It became stronger and stronger, until the whole chamber was bathed in a crimson color.

Nadan could now see the cavern they were in clearly. It was a roughly made catacomb with rust stone walls that stretched for numerous paces around them, nothing like the geometrically designed crypts of Simkada with their polished walls and patterned, domed ceilings. The walls were unfinished and jag-ged. Here and there, long shelves, filled with large gems and small books, stretched along the rock wall. The floor beneath them was covered with some type of resinous-smelling straw or bark.

"Are all these ajnir writings?" asked Nadan. He estimated, just by scanning the shelves quickly, that there were at least 400 scrolls or books in the lair.

Cropaayaa was walking slowly along the rows of books, scanning the aisles, his head tipped over to one side at an angle to view the bindings of the books.

"Just a few," he said, after a second's hesitation as he pulled a small red book from the shelf. "Most of these books are collectibles from different parts of the city."

"Do you have any arthanti here?" asked Nadan, suddenly. The thought had just occurred to him. Nadan was surprised it hadn't sooner.

"I'm not sure what you mean by that word," said Cropaayaa, looking at him sharply. "But I sense that you mean the gems that send you into other realms."

"Yes."

"We have one such gem," said Cropaayaa. "Not all guntaras know of it."

He paused for a moment, then said: "I have a sense about you."

"A sense?" asked Nadan.

"Yes, I cannot say exactly what it is," said Cropaayaa. "But I cannot escape the feeling somehow that you are like Glonerat in some way. You know him, of course?"

"He was from the ancient world, my teacher told me," said Nadan. "They say he could turn leaves of grass into gold or silver with metas and that he single-handedly defeated a kaitone beast outside of Valyna. But how could you know what Glonerat was like?"

"I've read all his writings in this vault. They have become part of my being. Even as I have read them, I feel like I've known the great ajnir, as if he sits in front of me, speaking in flesh and blood." Cropaayaa handed him the small red book. "This is the only writing we have about the uriel," the man said. "About 10 years ago, some of our guntaras went around the city, interviewing people who had such experiences and documenting what they heard."

Nadan scanned through the book quickly, thumbing through the pages. The book was mainly just a collection of reports on the phenomenon with a familiar thread: strange, morphing figures, appearing in the night, that spoke unusual riddles. But something was uniquely different about the sightings of the uriel: the messages people got were clearer.

He wondered if people had imagined it some, but many of the riddles were surprisingly intelligible. One, for example, reported the being saying to a young girl: *Your thoughts are an illusion. And yet your people think I am an illusion.* The author remarked that the girl was too young and uneducated yet to even entertain thoughts of that caliber. However, the authors came to no conclusion at the end of the book, as to what the uriels may be.

"What has been your conclusion about the uriel, after all your study of the phenomenon?" Nadan finally asked, closing the book.

Cropaayaa was polishing his telescoping glasses with a piece of blue silk. Naria and Ranum were milling around the cavern, peering into different books on the shelves.

"I have reached no conclusion," the man said. "We have seen an influx in the amount of the experiences, since people began to see the flashes of light over the Great Fault. It has led many scientists to conjecture, like many others across Urshan Dai, that the sightings are electrically induced. I think there is probably a linkage between the two occurrences, but I'm certain the flashes of light over the Fault do not originate from any phenomenon we currently understand."

"Have you ever seen a uriel yourself?" asked Naria, coming over after hearing their discussion.

"I have not talked to one," said Cropaayaa, taking on an official, scientific air in his speech. "But, several years ago, I had a strange experience which awakened my interest in the subject. I was sitting on the edge of the Fault one winter evening, when I saw what seemed to be a small, luminous figure walking in the void of space out over the Fault. As I watched, I saw another luminous figure join it and disappear over my head to the east in a single instant. Since then, I have tried to learn everything I can about the uriel."

"Can't you ask the Watching for the answers?" asked Ranum. "I'm not very good at that, but I think one of you could figure this out."

Nadan sensed the frustration in his friend's voice. Ranum didn't like prolonged mysteries of this sort.

"Well, you are a bit more hasty than your friend, I see," observed Cropaayaa. "The Quiescent state, as you call it, or the Jaloopaa as we call it in Mandi, doesn't yield answers to things beyond the scope of this universe. Dinjin has a similar intuitive state of mind, but its functioning is entirely different from anything in our universe. In our world, we connect to the intuition through a perceptive state of feeling. In Dinjin and perhaps other universes, the beings there connect through a different, more cerebral state of mind, an awareness that reaches beyond the emotions. It is difficult to describe. So that is your answer, perhaps."

Cropaayaa stopped, as a moth flew across the lumin-globe for a moment. Ranum fumbled with the red book, which he had taken from Nadan, examining the strange Mandian dialect closer.

"Well, it is good to find others who share my interest," Cropaayaa said, at length. "There are not many, even among us ajnir, who actually take an interest in the subject. There is the Yazax group, the subculture that believes the messages have hidden meaning. But they are not ajnir I have read their interpretations of the sayings, but I am not inclined to believe them. I wonder: How is that you three have come to have such an interest?"

"I was led here by a uriel," said Nadan.

Cropaayaa paused and stared at the handheld lumin-globe attached to his finger. Nadan could tell he was surprised, even though his stoic features weren't revealing it.

"What made you believe it was giving you good advice?" the man said after a moment.

"I was doubtful at first, but an elder ajnir in Simkada advised to me do what it said," said Nadan. "He advised me this way because my teacher, Manalk, had spoken with a uriel and actually came to believe their sayings had some value and meaning."

"That's unusual advice, but Manalk is not unknown in these parts," said Cropaayaa. "I did not know him personally, but I had heard of him. He was known for having great powers of insight. I had heard he was banished to Mazag."

Nadan said nothing, looking at the floor despondently.

Another silence fell over the conversation. Finally, Nadan broke it. His voice trembled as he spoke. He had not spoken to anyone before about his experience in the Dark Realm in Valyna. For some reason, giving words to it made him anxious, as if he were summoning a black spirit into the room with them.

"I went into the depths of the Order myself," he said. "I found a gem, the arthanti that connects one to the Dark Realm."

Cropaayaa's face became visibly disturbed.

"It would drive most insane, they say," the man said.

"There's more," said Nadan. "I was able to penetrate into that world, and I was able to telepath with Manalk, my teacher. I appeared physically in that world actually, though they said I could not."

"That's impossible," said Cropaayaa.

"I do not know how I was able to do it, but it happened," said Nadan, feeling suddenly weary. The thought of that place, with the images now reeling through his mind, was depressing to him.

Cropaayaa studied Nadan's eyes for almost a minute. *You speak the truth*, Cropaayaa telepathed to him. It was their most convenient way of communicating, so deep was the man's presence immersed in Nadan's psychology.

I thought you guntaras never invaded the thoughts of others, responded Nadan, with a smile.

"We do, here and there," said Cropaayaa. "Sometimes, we use it when words feel useless."

"I would like to look into the arthanti you have here," said Nadan. "I wonder if I could return to Haalathrom with it."

"I'm not sure. I usually just see a place filled with vegetation, a lush forest for a while. The plants are all different colors. There is a woman I meet there sometimes named Luspen."

Cropaayaa went over to the shelf at the far end of the cavern and returned with a small gem in his hand. It looked exactly like the one Nadan had used in Simkada, except this one was red.

"This is the arthanti I have in my possession," the old man said. "Normally, we would restrict ajnir that have not been properly trained, for safety reasons, of course. But, since you have already touched such a gem twice, Nadan, I would not forbid you from doing so. If you touched the Mazag gem, I cannot imagine this would be much more difficult."

Nadan thought about this for a moment, rubbing his fingers across his chin. He remembered the strange experience almost a year ago when he had seen the Ancient Sleeper's tomb and that ring of grass and that strange-looking forest. It was only for a moment he had seen that world, but it had changed his awareness completely. Again, he felt the strange, scintillating energy of the arthanti he had felt that day in Manalk's cave when he had first touched it, but the quality of the attraction was distinctly different than the one he had with this gem. This one felt more airy, like ideas running quickly along on an endlessly shifting stream.

Cropaayaa opened his wrinkled palms, extending the gem on both hands toward Nadan. "Don't press it too hard," he cautioned.

For some reason, Nadan felt anxious, as if something monumental were about to happen. Even as he touched the gem, Cropaayaa's face became blurry, faded, and ghost-like; he saw a blade of white grass trickle across his vision. Then, he heard a rumbling sound that softened to an ethereal wind in his ears.

The next moment, he was in a different world.

Chapter 16

Luspen

The trees that hemmed Nadan in on all sides possessed a metallic gold color. They were tall and thin, with huge trunks that got wider at the top and skinnier at the base. The wind-like roaring in his eardrums subsided, and the forest was silent, except for a dim clinking sound, like a bird pecking on metal. The trees swayed in the strong breeze, causing three of them to bend over so sharply that Nadan thought they were going to fall over. Even as he feared they were going to snap, they abruptly changed to the color of silver and moved back to their previous positions.

The atmosphere was dim but less so than the time he had been on the planet Haalathrom. He wasn't sure if this was the same planet, but it didn't appear similar. He controlled his emotions, reciting a mind-calming meta to himself. Even as he did so, he heard something rustling in the grass next to him. He looked up and saw a figure of a woman.

"Why do you change the color of my trees?" said the woman, calmly. "I prefer them the color of gold, but you are frightened. I suppose that is understandable."

"What is this world I am in?" he asked, hesitantly. He was feeling confused but surprisingly calm, like the first time he had been in the Dinjin.

"This is Tern'an, my planet," she said. "I am Luspen, you see, and I am its planet keeper." She stooped and picked a blade of silver grass at her feet. It instantly turned the color of blue in her palm.

"How did you know I was here?"

"I was just flying on the rhythms of light in those trees overhead, when I was called into form by your thought. You wanted to see me, so I appeared."

He glanced at Luspen's face and saw that words, written in some strange, dark alphabet, were flowing from her mouth. "What are those words in the air?" he asked.

"An incantation. It makes our world more wholesome, you see. You have upset it with your presence somewhat."

After a moment, the trees and their leaves returned again to their gold color. Her white arms moved upward in a Y-shape, then fell back to her side. She was wearing no clothes at all, but she was standing behind some rose-colored shrubs that disguised most of her body. Her white skin peered through the branches and stems. Her long black hair lay infinitely still as he looked at her.

"The trees change colors like this because your direct-knowledge capacity is ruffled," explained Luspen. "You see: the foliage has become gold and comfortable again because you are calmer. If your thoughts became jumbled again, the trees would turn silver, or even black, a lower color on the spectrum of thought. This world mirrors your thoughts more acutely than your world. It happens in your dimension, too, but it is much less obvious.

"Quiet your thoughts for a moment and concentrate on me," she added, after a moment.

Nadan focused on Luspen's form for almost a minute. Gradually, he felt his consciousness rising into the atmosphere; the dimness of the air subsided into a splendorous wave of clarity. He was soon above the trees, on top of a golden rooftop of vegetation, overlooking a green sky into which his mind was moving endlessly. A sense of bliss began simmering within him.

"So you wish to know what the uriel are?" asked Luspen.

"I have been wishing to know."

"The strange apparitions your people have been seeing come from the other half of your planet," said Luspen.

Luspen's voice held a deep stillness, which brought Nadan quickly into new thought patterns. Nadan felt that same monumental sense of gravity he had felt moments ago with Cropaayaa, as if a profound gong had chimed in the air next to him, vibrating through his being. All his attention turned from the surroundings to the woman before him. He suddenly felt depressed. The trees around him turned a slightly charcoal shade. He sat down on the fallen trunk of a silver tree, which was lying behind him. Luspen raised her arms again; the trees returned to the color of gold.

"The life forms of our world are more sensitive to energy than those in your world," she said. "Those anxious thoughts you have disturb the health of these trees, you see. But do not worry about it."

"That is interesting," he said, trying to feel more positive. "You say the uriel come from the other side of our planet, but where is the other half of our planet?"

Luspen looked at him fondly. He felt the same energy of bliss move through his being.

"This has also been a great mystery on your planet for centuries, I know," she said. "To solve this thing is what you are coming to me for, you see. The other side of the planet, this Eroma, as you call it, is in a limbo state between Dinjin and your universe, you see. It actually has never moved, in one sense. It is still there, connected to your planet, but it is invisible to you and your people, because you have not the vision to see Dinjin, except with the aid of these gems. The best of you can only sense it, you see."

As Nadan thought this over, it suddenly made sense to him. Korbluun had said the planet was never rocked from its orbit. This would explain why. When he looked over at Luspen again, he noticed she had disappeared.

"But how can a planet just slip into another universe?" he asked. He wasn't sure if she was still within hearing range.

I am needed elsewhere right now, she telepathed back to him. *But that has to do with your planet keeper, Talili, the keeper of Urshan Dai, you see. It is not well known, but the planet keepers adapt to the will of their inhabitants. When they change, they evolve or devolve with them. In the case of your planet, the other side of your planet, Eroma, evolved differently thousands of years ago than the side you currently dwell on. Eroma dwellers were very close to Dinjin in themselves, while the other side was less motivated to seek it.*

They preferred working the earth and developing technology, while Eroma dwellers liked to live in nature and feel the Dinjin. After a while Talili became uncomfortable with the Eroma side of her planet—it was more her nature to work with the material dimension—so she assigned a new planet keeper from the Dinjin, Zalaam, to oversee Eroma. But a war broke out between the two sides of the planet, and Zalaam and Talili both leapt to the defense of their respective people. To end the war, Zalaam shifted Eroma into the Dinjin slightly, but not fully, his native reality.

Talili. Nadan murmured the name to himself. The word felt vaguely familiar on his tongue, as did many of the ajnir words.

"But you said the other half of the planet was in some sort of limbo?" he asked, after reflecting on this carefully.

Yes, it is part of Dinjin now, but not as fully as the planet we are on now. It would seem blurry to the inhabitants of this planet. It became a shadow planet. You see, Nadan, some of the inhabitants of the other half of your planet wanted Dinjin, but they didn't want it fully, only partly. For that reason, some of the planet remains in your universe, partly affecting it. That is why the place you call Kira Mandi is so close to Dinjin. It is the closest point of contact with our universe and the other half of your planet, which is buried within Dinjin. In fact, the other half of the planet never really went anywhere in the way that your people commonly understand it.

Luspen reappeared near him suddenly, wearing a brown skin robe and carrying a small animal, with a tentacle protruding from its head. He had seen this animal once before.

"An omisat," he said.

"Yes, you have already met one of my pets, you see," she said, stroking the creature fondly. "Laki. There aren't many on your planet, but they come from Tern'an. I send them there from time to time, you see. He was upset by your presence, and I had to catch him."

The golden canopy darkened, as if a thundercloud had moved over it. The scene around him became splotchy, like a static-filled screen.

"I'm fading from this world," Nadan said.

Luspen moved toward him quickly and touched his arm, then quickly withdrew it. A warm radiance suddenly touched Nadan's being, and the scenery became lucid again.

"That should keep you in this world for a little longer," Luspen said.

Nadan sat down in the grass, running his apparition hands through it over and over. A singing sound was in the air, like an electronic humming sound but more soothing and organic. He felt delighted that he could stay in this world a little longer. It was a strange place and altogether foreign, but Nadan had the feeling that it was in some way his home.

"There is still another question you wished to ask me," said Luspen.

"Yes, I was wondering why a uriel has led me all this way," he said. "I don't know if it was the same one every time, but more than once one has told me that Kira Mandi is my home."

"That is because it is your home."

"But I was born and raised in Simkada."

"You were also born thousands of years ago in Kira Mandi."

The colors of the trees and grass around Nadan turned suddenly bluish-orange. He quieted his mind. The trees gradually returned to the golden hue, matching the plants that surrounded Luspen. He said nothing in response.

"Many thousands of years ago, before the planet split in two, you were living in Kira Mandi," explained Luspen. "You and your family lived on the far eastern side of the city, among the people of Urshan Dai who were more drawn to Dinjin. As the border between Zalaam's and Talili's domains crossed in the middle of the city, Kira Mandi was a divided city then, and there was much turmoil. You would rarely visit the other side of the city, for fear of violence.

"But, one day, there was a festival on the other side of the city, and you and your friends decided to travel to the east side of the city. You went for several hours. When you decided to return home, to your utter sorrow and dismay, the other half of the city and the planet had disappeared. You were dumbstruck with grief. Your entire family had disappeared, and you now had no one left, except a few of your friends. You lay for days on the edge of the planet, not eating, your heart lifeless with grief. So great was your grief that you exited your body. You entered Dinjin and spoke with your family there. When you returned, you had become the first ajnir, Gooriom, one who treads between the universes. Ever since, it has been your dream to reconnect the planet again. That is why the uriel, your light companion, has led you to this place, so that you might fulfill this dream."

"Gooriom," said Nadan. "But I thought he was just legend."

Manalk had once told him about Gooriom, the first ajnir, but few details about the ancient seer existed. Some in the Wheel of Thought believed he was just a folklore hero who never existed. Manalk never told him exactly what he thought about the existence of the ancient seer.

Meanwhile, the colors of the trees and plants around him had turned to a mix of colors: bands of green, gold, blues, and crimson traced across his vision, mirroring his confusion. It was like the first time Manalk had told him he was an ajnir. He didn't want this greatness thrust upon him, but he knew he could not deny it, no more than he could deny the quivering, buoyant reality of the alternate universe around him.

Luspen stood looking at him calmly, with incandescent blue eyes.

"You don't have to worry about responsibility," she said, almost blithely.

"But I don't understand how I can pull the planet back to itself," said Nadan.

"You don't have to," said Luspen. "That is already happening. That is what the ajnir have been doing unwittingly for centuries. Every time an ajnir acts, every time he or she connects to Dinjin, Urshan Dai becomes closer to its other half, and Talili becomes more and more similar to her counterpart, Zalaam. At this moment in history, they are almost on the same level of being. That is why the uriel have been slipping through into your world again with more frequency. There are some, companions of your people on those planets, who also wish to see the planet reunified, and they have decided to slip through the pores of the universes and assist the ajnir of your

world. Their messages are distorted in the movement between universes, as is their appearance."

Nadan said nothing, digesting this. Luspen
seemed to suddenly hover over the ground, like a
luminescent insect. Confusion washed over Nadan,
and the plants around him this time turned the color
of orange. He was filled with the feeling that he
should travel to Eroma, somehow, if there was a way.

"You felt that," said Luspen. "That is good. That's
the next step."

With the omisat still in her hand, she lightly
"tapped him on the forehead with her index finger. The next instant, he was back in the cavern.
Cropaayaa, Naria, and Ranum were standing around
him in a circle.

Chapter 17

Gooriom

Tell us what you saw," said Naria.

She was now sitting on a stone chair, next to the table in the cavern where Nadan had been standing. Nadan's legs were wobbling slightly.

"I need to sit down," he said.

Naria stood up and, straightening the hem of her robe with her small hands, stepped aside, so Nadan could sit down. Once he was seated, he felt better. His ears were still thrumming with a profusion of sounds: an oceanic roar, chiming gongs, a bee-like humming sound.

Nadan began speaking, but he felt his tongue catch in his throat, even as he opened his lips. It wasn't so much that the experience was indescribable as it was an aversion to verbalizing it.

"It is better that the Dinjin be conveyed through Mind Streaming," said Cropeayaa. "It was always better that way with us."

A silence fell over the room, while they all concentrated on Nadan's immediate memories. Minutes passed, while Nadan relayed mentally the images to them of that world, the golden leaves, the morphing coloration effect, Luspen's silent form. He unfolded the startling and revealing dialogue he had had with the planet keeper, which drew slight, wispy gasps from all present except Cropaayaa.

"Gooriom," the old man muttered, finally. "So the legend is true."

"What legend?" asked Nadan.

"It is said among the ajnir of Kira Mandi that Gooriom would return someday, traveling from a distant city to bring the planetary pieces back to one another," he said.

Cropaayaa sat down on a stone chair, opposite Nadan, stroking his braided chin beard. Nadan looked at the ajnir. He was still having trouble seeing himself as an ancient seer. In a way, part of him detested the idea, almost the same way he did not want to be an ajnir at first.

"There is also an ajnir order in Kira Mandi?" he asked.

"Yes, it's known as the Gloehund Council, in memory of the guntara who founded it 41,000 years ago," said Cropaayaa. "They are like the Order of Valyna in some respects, which does not acknowledge our Council, but it is not so authoritative nor nearly so influential."

Even as Cropaayaa spoke, Nadan noticed that the sound in his ears had suddenly faded. All around the old ajnir's white hair, he could see different colored anamatis, thought particles moving and circling in the air. He hadn't witnessed the strange, phosphorescent phenomenon since he had first met Manalk. This time, the colors and movements of the tiny mental beams surged in the air with a powerful intensity. Instead of dripping and flitting about, they were moving, almost striding through the air, like tiny, confident beings.

"Do you see them?" he asked, with awe, pointing his finger toward the wall.

"What?" asked Ranum.

"The lights. The anamatis. They are so much brighter now."

"Yes, they are stronger in Kira Mandi than any-where else on our planet," said Cropaayaa. "We have studied this phenomenon in some detail as well. You should go to Istandria. They say the anamatis there are strongest."

Nadan pulled his eyes from the swirling lights and looked at the ajnir. He suddenly felt reluctant to take action. Even if he found some way to jump between the universes, he didn't want to go just yet. Now, he suddenly felt a deep longing to jour-ney to Eroma, perhaps as a result from his memory of his former life. He wanted to see Dinjin and the shadow planet. But he felt a strange repulsion from the idea as well. Cropaayaa seemed to sense his thought.

"Mazag," Cropaayaa muttered.

"Why do you speak of that place?" Nadan said.

"It is muddying your mind," said the ajnir.

Nadan glanced at Naria. Her faced appeared deep and complex to him.

"You are confused," he said.

"I'm wondering what will happen if Eroma planet returns," said Naria. "What will happen to our world, I wonder?"

"I could go back and ask Luspen again," said Nadan. "I did not think of the question."

"Luspen will answer no more questions at the moment," said Cropaayaa, mysteriously toying with his chin beard.

Ranum moved slowly along the wall, studying the rows of gems, humming to himself an old Simkadan tune. The sound of the old song that Nadan used to hear the Drogham sing in the spring outside his street relaxed his mind, transporting him momentarily to the place of his birth. The sound, cadent and light, felt strange, however. He sensed an odd juxtaposition between the music with this foreign environment, which seemed deeply sad and had no springtime. Even as the last note fell, twining in the air off Ranum's lips, Nadan felt a new energy surging through his heart, overwhelming the remnants of the past. It had been months now since he had first felt the change which Manalk had told him about, but the prescient emotion was now more vivid and powerful.

I believe Eroma's and Urshan Dai's evolutions are woven together, he murmured to Naria telepathically.

Chapter 18

Istandria

Hours later, a dark nimbus cloud had shrouded the city landscape overhead. The streets of Kira Mandi were bustling with crowds and merchants as usual, but they seemed to Nadan to be moving in almost slow motion, as if the sensation of time in this place had suddenly slowed to a halt. Bits of paper and dust were spiraling in the wind, out across the street and up onto the roofs of the kaaraadruun huts where Nadan and his friends were standing.

"Should we stay here, until it passes over?" asked Nadan.

"No, we can take my skiff," said Cropaayaa, distractedly. "It has a canopy."

They had decided to travel to Istandria for the rest of the day. Cropaayaa had mentioned the place, and Nadan felt an irresistible attraction to the place, and, an hour ago, a uriel had visited in the cavern below Cropaayaa's home, whispering the location in his ear, as well as some other unintelligible words he couldn't interpret. Istandria was a wealthy suburb of Kira Mandi, and it bordered the lonely, jagged mountain range, the Kliomas, that traversed the desert to the north of the metropolis. The villa stood 4,000 feet above Kira Mandi and offered a wide panoramic view of the mountains and the Gortag, which made it a major attraction to wealthy landowners and tourists.

Cropaayaa went around the back of his house and emerged a few minutes later, steering a sleek, jet-black anti-gravity skiff that sputtered every minute or so, exhaling black acron soot.

"It needs some work, but it will get us there," he remarked.

The storm rumbled and writhed off to the east. The sound of bird wings and croaking animal voices churned overhead. Nadan looked up. The flocks of birds above were white, spotted animals, with blue circles surrounding each of their large, bulbous eyes. Nadan immediately recognized them as the uyapa birds that roved the eastern desert. He had never seen them in such numbers before.

"The storm doesn't seem like it will run into our path, but I think we should take the skiff anyway," said Cropaayaa. "It will save us some time."

All four of them got up onto the skiff, with the old ajnir at the helm. Even as Nadan sat down, he felt a weight growing in his chest, like a leaden fist was pulling his heart into the earth. He fell forward for an instant, as the weight changed to a stabbing pain. His temples throbbed, and he felt dizzy.

"You are in pain," said Cropaayaa.

The torment suddenly passed. Nadan felt the air coursing through his lungs.

"I'm better," he said. "I think it was something from Mazag."

"That gargul has been following you ever since you entered the city," he said. "That is something different, though. It comes from Talili. She is upset with you."

Nadan eyed him with sudden curiosity.

"How do you speak to the ruler of this planet?" he said.

"I do not know. But I can feel her wrath in the earth."

Cropaayaa pushed the lever forward, and the skiff lurched forward, sharply. The skiff emitted a low, droning sound, like that of a bumblebee, but it was not completely silent, like the craft they had taken from Valyna.

As they moved along through the city, the low engine of the skiff droning and purring softly, Nadan couldn't help but notice again the profound mental silence that permeated the city, as if every-thing were moving more slowly. He looked at the countenances of merchants and women and chil-dren as they moved past. The sunlight had come out again, but they appeared inward and quiet, dis-engaged from their normal activities. He saw none of them chatting and laughing as before. Cropaayaa sped up the skiff, and their faces moved past in a blur. They soon arrived in the poorer section of the city, where the beggars lined the streets and where the people seemed wrapped in some introspective cocoon of quietness, a kind of silent trance. None of them held out their hands, crying in their strange accents for a cagma or a slice of bread. Still, Nadan felt a certain pity for them and dropped some of the coins from his pocket onto the street. None of the beggars flocked to the site where the coins had been dropped as usual, but he saw one young girl, clothed in dirty rags, stoop down to pick them up, one by one. Nadan looked around the city, feeling its soul, its collective mind. The city lay in a kind of mental stasis, paused in time, indifferent to commotion and the day cycle. It was like everything was hovering for a moment, waiting, tense, similar to just moments ago, when he had felt the deafening silence in the air.

"What is happening?" asked Nadan, after a few moments.

Cropaayaa murmured something to himself inaudibly, then said: "The silent moments. After they're done, people seem to forget about them and move on with their lives."

This talk left all of them reflective for a long moment, as Cropaayaa wove the skiff gradually through the dense, silent, immobile crowds. Nadan let his mind spread deeper into the awareness around him. The quietness was unearthly, like the result of some god's mind hushing its uncomprehending, less intelligent children. For a moment, he imagined the stillness sweeping across the desert, thousands of miles across, and filling the planet, spreading across it like a transparent film of oil. He saw this as a potential future, not a destiny, but a seed-idea waiting to sprout into form. Then, this visionary wave of thought vanished, the moment elapsed, and the crowds began seething and talking again, as if nothing had happened.

"It is gone," said Cropaayaa. "The moments are always transient, never lasting for more than a few minutes."

They kept moving along the street, not speaking, as they went. The crowds and the high, spiraling kaaraadruun huts soon ended abruptly. They were on the same street that led to Jakelpiodies, but instead of following the street toward the path, Cropaayaa banked the skiff and turned down a small dirt path that led into a small canyon, with steep walls and rows of red-leafed bushes, each with a large white flower sprouting at the top.

Nadan reached out with his hand and plucked some of the leaves, then cupped them in his hand so he could smell them. Their scent was sour but mildly aromatic. His heart was beating rapidly for some odd reason. He sat down, tossed the leaves off the skiff, and watched them skitter away across some mounds of sand they were passing.

"Are there many people that live in Istandria?" he asked.

"Not many. It's a small villa of influential people who do not speak Mandian but a variation of the dialect," said Cropaayaa. "They are said to be descended from Anatami."

Even as he looked down the road they were travelling, Nadan could feel the compelling magnetism of Istandria again. Somehow, he felt whatever he was supposed to do in Kira Mandi lay there for some inexplicable reason.

Cropaayaa was now picking his teeth with a splinter of Kurieme wood, while he stared at the compass. "Istandria is a great historic site, filled with many caves and catacombs," said Cropaayaa, picking up on Nadan's thought. "Many of the runes inside the cave stretch back thousands of years, even before Kira Mandi's history. The locals there regard the caves with interest and intrigue. But they do not see it the same way we guntaras do. We often bring young guntaras there for training. It is easier for them to feel Dinjin there. That may be what you are feeling."

They stopped talking, and the skiff moved silently and swiftly along the straight desert path, which had become barren and lifeless. There were no trees or vegetation of any kind on each side of them, and the color of the sand was purplish-red. It had a blaring intensity, causing Nadan to shield his eyes, as they went along. Cropaayaa sped the craft up faster.

Soon, Nadan fell asleep, dozing off to the gentle rocking of the skiff, huddled on the deck of the anti-gravity skiff, with his back against the bronze-colored platform at his head. He awoke to Naria nudging him on the shoulder. "We've arrived," she said, but her voice seemed worried.

Nadan got up, raising himself on the bronze deck, and surveyed the scene around them. They had stopped in a shallow dip in the road, with two large tower-like reddish stones leaping up on each side of them. A large black metal gate stood between the two towering stones. At the foot of the gate, Cropaayaa was standing in the shadows, talking to two men with gold hair, bleached by the sun, each carrying long spears. One of the man's faces kept twitching nervously from under his blue metallic helmet.

"I can see he is Simkadan, but the girl presents a problem," he said, waving his hand at Naria, who was sitting in the one of the skiff's metal seats still. "She is Valynan."

By the confident, self-assured tone of his voice, Nadan could tell the twitching was most likely hereditary, not due to any anxiety. As soon as he heard what the man had said, he began a trusting meta phrase in his mind, slowly and surely, letting it gather force within his mind.

"You must understand," said Cropaayaa. "We cannot leave one of our companions on the desert here. We simply wish to see the great ruins, nothing more. Our intent is not to spy."

The man's face became suddenly placid, as if he had controlled his facial muscles. "We have our laws," he said, flatly.

Nadan could sense that Ranum wanted to use his paralysis metas on the guards again, like in the city, but in his mind, he held his friend back. The guard with the twitchy face, who was apparently in charge, had become warm and friendly suddenly; his dense, black eyes, normally fixated and serious, softened. He looked at Nadan, then Naria for a moment. "Gao, open the gate for the visitors," said the man.

"You know the code, Jakul," Gao, the other man, said, looking at him seriously.

The first man's face had stopped twitching and was now firm and silent. The other mumbled something in Mandian, shrugged, then walked over to the gate. Placing his spear against the rock surface, he pressed a lever inside the cliff wall. The gate creaked for a single instant, then opened, quickly and soundlessly.

The group piled back into the skiff, while the metal gates heaved and grated open. Beyond, they could see a green field of grass, scattered here and there with Kurieme trees.

"That is the best I have ever performed that meta," said Nadan, as they passed through the gate. The two soldiers were looking at another skiff skimming off in the distance to the east. "My mind feels more focused for some reason."

"We are close to Istandria," said Cropaayaa, as if his mind was in another world. "Your inner power grows here."

As they moved along the widened highway, the vegetation became dense and greener; the hills rolled and undulated here, and the grass lined the side of the road. They saw a herd of boar-like beasts grazing on one of the hills, an animal Nadan recalled in Mandian was called a yul. After a mile or so, the dust-swept road they were on turned from red sand to yellowish clay brick.

"Are we leaving the Kiopic Desert?" asked Ranum.

"No," said Cropaayaa. "The village of Istandria rests over an oasis of water that flows underneath the ground. Pipes from this place run all the way to Kira Mandi, supplying all its people, so it is never in need of water."

They soon came to the village itself, a small enclave of high-domed huts and red stone walkways and gilded-robed residents walking along the streets. As they looked, Nadan could see that huts were elaborate and lavish, with several tiers, reminiscent of some of the aristocratic streets in Valyna.

"For centuries, Istandria has been a reservoir for the most wealthy residents of Kira Mandi," explained Cropaayaa.

"You would think that with all this water, a city would grow up on top of this place," remarked Ranum.

"It has been tried several times," said Cropaayaa. "But Istandria has a distinct and separate political government from that of Kira Mandi. The politicians of Istandria have long sought to keep the place from developing. It is ironic. Istandria means 'valley of poor' in the ancient dialect of Mandi. When this area of the planet was covered in forest and lakes thousands of years ago, it was the place where the destitute came to live off the land."

"Are we close to the ancient ruins?" asked Nadan.

"They are nearer to the Fault, away from the village," said Cropaayaa, waving his wrinkled hand toward the east. "It will be a few minutes before we reach them."

They came to an intersection, where a white, marble road ran perpendicular to the gravel road they were travelling. It was perfectly straight and narrow, slicing through the gullies and ravines into the west with flat, even precision.

"The Calaiuuma Tera, the white road," said Cropaayaa. "It is the oldest street on our planet, built some 50,000 years ago, before the Great Fault appeared. It is said the road ran straight from the center of Istandria to another city, which was lost when the planet split."

Calaiuuma. The word didn't sound as familiar to Nadan as the sight of the white avenue, piercing through the verdant landscape. *Perhaps it was called a different name back then, when I was here,* he thought. For he knew now that he had been here before, as if he had seen this place thousands of times already in his dreams.

Cropaayaa paused at the intersection, then banked the skiff around, proceeding slowly along the marble street. As they went along, they enjoyed the scent of vegetation, a smell none of them had experienced since they had left Valyna. Kira Mandi had no gardens or vegetation, except a few scattered desert species that pockmarked the streets and balconies here and there. They soon came to a wooded area with small pafnegu trees whose white trunks were spaced evenly, almost in rows, in the short yellow grass that skirted around their bases. The trees were smaller than the ones Nadan was accustomed to seeing in Simkada.

"This is the only woodland west of Valyna," said Cropaayaa. "The politicians of Istandria planted this grove almost a decade ago. It has become a great attraction. Mandi politicians hope to do something similar inside their city shortly."

Cropaayaa quickened the pace of the skiff, and they moved rapidly through the small grove, the trees moving past them in a silent blur. When they reached the end of the grove, the vegetation and grassland ended abruptly, leading into a vast wasteland of sand and stones. Huge, monolithic rocks jutted up irately at the horizon line, rough hewn as if cut and tossed by some crazed divine being. Here and there, small patches of lime-colored grass protruded among the charcoal-colored stones. The landscape had become a barren desert again, a white, pristine river of stone through its heart. In the distance, to the northeast, they saw a triangular-shaped mountain, with steep shoulders and jagged edges funneling up to a broken, lopsided steeple.

In the distance, they heard a faint rumbling.

"The oasis ends here," said Cropaayaa. He pointed his long wizard-like finger at the mountain. "There is also Recuma, the great volcano. She has been sleeping for centuries, but she is awake again, as you can now hear."

The rumbling subsided, but Nadan still felt its aftershock mentally, within his being. The earth was angry, it seemed; he had felt this primeval emotion before in Simkada, the morning they had departed the city. But he also sensed something else there now, a fear, a trembling. The anger in the soil was less an overpowering, dominating sort of emotion than it was reactive, defensive, almost panicked.

Nadan said nothing of these thoughts to his companions, as they sped quietly along the pale road, but he could see they felt something was unusual about this place, too. Naria seemed agitated and was sitting in the back of the seat, watching the temple-like mountain with unblinking, placid eyes. The wind was blowing back her auburn hair. Finally, she regained her poise, drawing her porcelain hands around her slender shoulders to keep her cloak from flapping in the wind. Nadan noticed this gesture made her seem older than she was. For the first time since Nadan had met her, she looked like a woman, not a child, or as if this place had awoken some extraordinary deepness within her. But, in a paradoxical way, the deepness also made her seem more innocent and childlike. As he thought about it, it seemed to him that subtler, not older, was the right word for it. He wondered if she had always been this way.

Nadan sat down next to her, on the metal bench near the tail of the vehicle.

"You feel Talili's wrath," said Naria, to him.

She had perceived it even sooner than he had within himself. It was true. He could sense the planet keeper's vehemence toward him growing, mounting like the fire in the volcano's bowels off in the distance. Talili knew Nadan threatened her dominion. Or was it more than that? Did she see a future that he had not seen? Was there some adverse consequence of his action, which he hadn't perceived himself?

"Perhaps you will discover that answer in Dinjin, if you go there," said Naria. "I cannot see the future either, but I sense something."

She shuddered and looked glumly at the sand passing underneath them. A silence enveloped their conversation; side-by-side, they watched the brown, rust-colored landscape careening by them.

"You don't wish me to go, do you?" said Nadan, finally.

"I will miss you, but I do not challenge your fate," said Naria, looking mournfully at him. "But I wonder whether this is the only course."

"What other course might there be?"

Naria looked away from him but said nothing.

It took only a few minutes for them to pass over the flat desert and enter into the small, hilly terrain that surrounded the base of the volcano. The short, coarse shrubs grew densely on the steep, sandy slopes on either side of the path they had taken. Cropaayaa wound the skiff through the serpentine trail, until the hills suddenly dropped off and the path fell down a steep road into a valley. Proceeding down the slope, they could see the edge of the Great Fault clearly, a deep crevasse of stars, glazed over by a slight, wispy mist, where the eye expected landscape.

"Has anyone climbed down the Gortag, I wonder?" he said out loud. He had been sitting in the back of the skiff the whole time, being unusually quiet. The place, Nadan noticed, seemed to have a strange quieting effect on him.

"There have been many attempts," said Cropaayaa. "They have mostly died, though, and it's not often tried anymore. Kalam, a famous mountaineer, made it across the Gortag to Valyna once but never tried it again."

"Why did he never try again?" asked Ranum.

"Too many volcanoes," said Cropaayaa.

At the bottom of the valley, they saw a ragged circle of tall white stones, lying on top of one another and at angles, patterned obviously by some human intelligence. A yellow and white mist was swirling about the stones, imbuing them with eeriness. As they came into the center of the ring of stones, a man in an orange robe pulled his skiff up next to theirs, as Cropaayaa slowed his to a halt. Nadan could see the man's face easily now. He had gold hair, almost as shiny as Ranum's, but his eyebrows were white with age. One half of his dark skin was wrinkled; the other half was smooth, like a young child's.

Cropaayaa fell into speaking Mandian with the man for a few minutes. Nadan couldn't understand what they were saying, but he perceived the man was speaking in a different dialect than Cropaayaaa, who was having trouble understanding him. Nadan said a translation meta, murmuring the phrase Manalk had once taught him to help speak with foreigners. He caught the last part of the conversation, something about anamatis and the lights of the Gortag becoming stronger right now.

The conversation ended, and the man in the orange robe disappeared quickly into the mist.

"His name is Jali, a river reader, one of the tribe of Quilli," explained Cropaayaa. "The tribe lives out here, protecting the ruins, which they believe are their ancestral home. He was just making sure we weren't prowlers or thieves."

"Why was one side of his face wrinkled like that?" asked Nadan.

"No one knows, but all the Quilli have the same thing happen to them, when they age," said Cropaayaa. "Their children look normal, similar to any Mandian child. But as they get older, one side of their body shrivels; the other side remains youthful, until they die."

"Is that because they live closer to the Gortag?" asked Nadan.

Cropaayaa's black eyes glinted in the dull fog.

"That is one theory we have," he said, tossing his toothpick onto the ground near them.

"What's a river reader?"

"I see you were hearing with that meta of yours. Yes, they read the anamatis of rivers, the Quilli. That is what they like to do. They read the history of the planet that way."

Cropaayaa stepped out of the piloting seat of his skiff and onto the black sand. Ranum, Naria, and Nadan got down from the machine in turn. As soon as Nadan's feet were on the soft black soil, he felt a dagger-like point slice through his back. He cried out and fell to his knees on the sand. Cropaayaa ran to him, kneeling down. But by that time, Nadan was writhing in agony. Hundreds of tiny, invisible daggers felt like they were cutting through his flesh. Nadan looked down but didn't see himself bleeding. He felt the same apparition that had clung to him the night before in Kira Mandi, pulling on him again, this time with more intensity and vigor.

The planet will not come back, the being said, in Nadan's mind.

Cropaayaa held his palm out over Nadan's body for a moment.

"It is trying to cut his invisible being from his physical being," he murmured, anxiously.

Nadan heard the man's voice faintly, as if it were reverberating from an echo chamber, far off in the distance. Then, he felt his mind letting go of his physical form, drifting in spasms in rhythm with the pulls and yanks of the apparition. For a moment, he saw himself on the ground, with Cropaayaa standing around him, and Naria and Ranum standing on either side of him. Out of the mists above the Gortag, stars peeked through the curling fog. The stars became brighter, more lucid, clearer than anything he had ever seen. They shimmered, then dissipated from his sight, and then he found himself back in his body. A word was repeating itself in his mind: *Samaalcran*, a dispelling meta.

"I almost lost you," said Cropaayaa. Nadan realized the ajnir had been saying the meta over and over in his mind.

Nadan sat up. All the pain had left his limbs, and he heard a deep buzzing sound in his ears, a sound that was not physical.

"The being cannot enter into one of the catacombs, the sacred ruins," said Cropaayaa. "It knows that. It knew it was here that it had its last chance to pull you away forever into its world. We should enter the ruins quickly."

Cropaayaa helped Nadan to his feet. Nadan felt dizzy and sick, as if he might vomit. His legs were wobbling as he began to walk slowly toward the ruins. Nadan leaned on Ranum's shoulder, as they reached the edge of the ruins, which were actually closer to them than originally appeared. In front of them and above their heads was a sheer rock wall, which shot up mysteriously into the mist over their heads. Set inside the rock wall were three black iron doors spaced several feet apart.

"How do we get in?" asked Ranum.

Even as he asked the question, the door farthest on the left swung open noiselessly. A short, hooded figure stepped out, extending a long, wrinkled finger. The figure said nothing but waved its hand for them to follow, then walked back through the door.

"That's a weird way to welcome someone," muttered Ranum.

Cropaayaa stopped waving his arms back and forth and went toward the door.

"Her name is Pnav'Kle," he said. "She is observing a year of silence. It is the tradition of the Quilli to do so every seven years."

Even as he spoke, Nadan felt a cold breath stinging the nape of his neck and a hard, cruel, transparent hand clasping around his throat. But the hand withered away in the mist, its power vanquished. He was in a small, low passageway that curved in a gradual arc to the left. At the top of the ceiling, a row of tiny lumin-globes, yellow and red, stretched in even spaces along the length of the stone passageway, as far as he could see. He was standing next to a small table with a lumin-globe suspended above it which cast a pale blue electronic light on the polished surface of the table. Even as Nadan looked at it, he knew it was a mystical light, like nothing he had ever seen before. Pnav'Kle, an old woman, was staring up into it, her face barely visible in the faint glow of the cavern.

One side of her face was shriveled, an old woman's face; the other side was fresh and pretty, like a young girl's.

The doors behind them folded silently behind them.

The light from above opens and closes the doors, telepathed Cropaayaa. *The light is a living entity; it lets in those who it wants to.*

You want to cross over to Yaoliem, Pnav'Kle telepathed, walking over to him.

Nadan stepped back. The telepathing was crystal clear. He had never experienced the psychic force as so lucid before.

Yaoliem is their name for Dinjin, Cropaayaa telepathed, in explanation. *Do not speak out loud to her. It is considered taboo to draw a Quilli into conversation during their year-long observation.*

Nadan looked more intently at the woman. Her eyes were now mirthful, glittering as she perceived his thought. He had imagined someone who hadn't spoken for a year to be grim and lonely. On the other hand, she seemed more alive and aware than most ajnir he had met.

Pnav'Kle turned quickly and, waving her hand in the same way as before, began walking down the passageway, with soft, silent steps. The three travelers fell in behind their old ajnir guide, all walking silently along the stone path. The passageway was narrow at first, only allowing them to walk in single file, but soon it opened up into a wider space, allowing them to walk two abreast. As Nadan pulled up alongside Naria, he began to feel the first rumblings of a premonition in his mind. In it he heard the ruminations of many voices speaking in a language he could not understand. The voices carried a mixture of emotions—both sad and happy, painful and painless—but they seemed to emanate from some vast echo chamber in and all around him. The voices seemed to come from another dimension.

"Do you feel that, Naria?" Nadan whispered.

She shook her head sideways toward him, eyes askance.

"No," she said, finally. "What is it?"

"I felt many voices, calling to me," he said.

Ahead of them, Pnav'Kle paused for a short moment, as if listening to their thoughts, then kept walking. They followed her for several minutes, not speaking any further, until the flickering lumin-globes in the hallway gave way to darkness. They all stopped, while Pnav'Kle paused and lit a handheld lumin-globe in her hand and led them along the passageway, which was now descending steeply in tight, concentric circles. In a few minutes, they stopped descending; they found themselves in a wide hallway with massive black stone pillars, which loomed up gigantically in the foggy, damp mist that lay all about the place. Tall, hooded shapes of Quilli flitted about among the pillars, with lumin-globes waving back and forth in their hands. In the back of the cavern, they could hear the soft roar of water, the tinkle of small rivulets.

"This is the underground river of Lutisia," said Cropaayaa. "It is the main source of water for the village. The river has the highest number of anatamis on the planet. The river readers spend most of their time here."

They walked further into the hallway, which had a huge, arcing dome of a ceiling overhead. Cool air was circulating in the place, filling their nostrils with a fresh, aquatic scent. Nadan and Ranum walked to the far side to see the river, which snaked through the center of the cavern, brackish and murky. They saw several Quilli, dressed in red and black robes, crouched on the black, mossy bank of the river.

"What are they doing?" asked Nadan.

"They are looking for the anamatis of the river," said Cropaayaa, who was walking behind them without their noticing.

"I didn't know inanimate things could have thoughts," said Nadan.

"Yes, they do, but their thoughts are more subtle, more difficult to discern," replied Cropaayaa.

"And why are they looking for the thoughts of the river?" asked Ranum. He seemed perturbed for some reason, and Nadan couldn't seem to tell why.

"So they may know already what happened to the other part of our planet," said Nadan.

"It is likely, but the Quilli guard their knowledge, rarely telling the outside world of what they learn on these shores," said Cropaayaa. "They do, however, record it in their secret language, which they only teach to their own people. The arthanti use these symbols."

At that moment, one of the Quilli, a teenager who had no hair except for a black braid falling off the left side of his head, came over to Nadan from the edge of the river, where he had been hunched, peering into a churning pool of Kurieme leaves.

"The river is not right today," said the boy, in Nadan's own language. "I wouldn't call it angry, but it's disturbed. Black and red anamatis, mostly. Very strange, and not good colors together. It is a strange chapter of our planet I'm reading—about a war long ago, not sure when in Kira Mandi, and a king bewitching his son by mistake, and the son losing his mind."

"I would like to know how to read events and memory from anamatis," said Nadan. "But I can't imagine how to do so."

"It's not as hard as you think," said the boy. "If you keep staring intently at an anamati long enough and intently enough, pictures and events will start to unfold in your mind."

Nadan looked up at the pillar above his head, eyeing the rough, mossy, damp surface. He stepped toward it, feeling its surface with his palm. A slimy, black, algae-like vegetation was growing on its surface. The lumin-globe overhead suddenly flickered more brightly, and he noticed small indentations, inscribed in the stone, underneath the thin, transparent layer of algae.

"What are these, Cropaayaa?" he asked.

"Those are Quilli engravings on these walls," said Cropaayaa. "There is one on each pillar."

He stopped to telepath, and, after a few seconds, Pnav'Kle appeared around the edge of the pillar. She looked more refreshed than before, compared to when Nadan had last seen her, almost as if the watery air had revived her being. Suddenly, in that instant, he felt what she felt; there was a strong energy, an ajnir vibration mingling in the air and even in the stones. The presence was so subtle he hadn't noticed it before. But its imperceptibility didn't diminish its power. Nadan suddenly felt buoyant, as if he were floating on a wisp of mist or smoke. Again, he sensed strange, murky voices calling out to him, as if out of a cosmic echo chamber.

This one says: No location can be realized for those who journey across. The old crone was telepathing her translation of the phrase to them.

Nadan thought about it for a moment.

It sounds like directions of some sort, he replied back to her.

These are ancient adages for leaping into the other universe, Pnav'Kle telepathed back. *That is why I brought you here.*

She turned, and they followed her steps to the next pillar.

This one says: A universe is its own dream. A real dream of the other leads to the other.

A herd of five Quilli passed by, staring with insect-like eyes from under their hoods, as she moved past the second pillar and to the third, which was nearest the entrance from which they had come. It was the last pillar in the place. The algae were thick on the engraving, and Nadan had to wipe the coating off with his fingers to read the symbols below it.

It says: Each universe is within us, telepathed Pnav'Kle. *When this is actualized, travel becomes easy.*

With the reading of the last message in his thoughts, Nadan suddenly felt a deep rushing sound, like a voiceless wind in his ear. It was like a memory, the comprehension that now overtook him, a distant but gradually deepening memory. He suddenly realized that he was expanding his mind further than he had ever thought possible. He realized he had to dream another dream; he had to make Dinjin more real to him than just a thought or an energy field within him. Even as he had the thought, he felt his mind moving across the glinting, damp stones, out into the sand, into the volcano, Recuma, and into the villages and cities. He went deeper, out into the Kiopic Desert, to Valyna and to his homeland, Simkada. His mind was about to move into space beyond the planet Urshan Dai, when he felt a forceful pressure on his wrist. His mind returned to his corporeal form immediately, and he saw it was Naria, holding his hand in her soft white palms. Her skin was cold and damp against his. She was shivering.

"Stop," she said. "You must not go yet."

She was on the verge of tears. Ranum came up behind her with a sad, almost depressed expression on his face.

"How long will you be gone?" asked Naria, finally controlling herself.

"I do not know," said Nadan. "Do not grieve. I have a sense I will be back."

Ranum fidgeted and then spoke.

"Where will you return?" he said. "Might you decide to end up in Simkada again?"

I don't know, telepathed Pnav'Kle.

"Very well," said Ranum. "We will stay here until your return."

With that, Ranum walked over and hugged Nadan. Naria followed, embracing him for a long moment. She had controlled her tears, but she still looked despondent.

"I just had a strange feeling you would not return," said Naria. "As if you were dying, almost. It has passed now."

She laughed, with jitters in her voice.

"Perhaps, in one way, I may be dying," said Nadan, reflectively.

He turned to Pnav'Kle, relaying to her a silent message of farewell. Then, he bowed low to Cropaayaa, in Mandian fashion.

"I will watch over your friends, until your return," said Cropaayaa.

There was a happiness and steady detachment in his voice. Nadan felt comforted by it. He was touched by his friends' sadness, but it almost felt like a weight upon his departure. He looked at them all for one long last moment, smiling. A sudden, blazing thought, like a uriel's riddle, probed into his mind: *This dream will melt into another dream.*

Then, he returned his mind to the quiescent, expansive state. He felt the Dinjin tingling in the air here, as if it were an eager travel companion waiting for him. Space, the wheeling stars and moons in Urshan Dai's solar system, was also waiting, it seemed; he felt time slipping away, his mind stretching out into the infinity of galaxies. The expanse around him was so great it almost terrified him, but, as he embraced it entirely with his being, he heard a single word in his mind, like a resounding gong: *isnan,* the word for freedom in Mandian.

Time paused, holding its lush, endless breath of ideas and events. He was part of it all, not separate. *I have never in my life been awake until now,* he thought.

THE END

Glossary

acron – the fuel for anti-gravity skiffs that is mined below Valyna

Ajnir, ajnir – means *secret worker* in the language of Ganir; one who has been "awakened" and is directly in contact with the Dinjin, a higher dimension of reality

anamatis – thought particles, which flow between the three universes and shuttle the thoughts of telepaths and other beings back and forth between each other

Anatami – a supposedly extinct tribe of desert people on Urshan Dai

appaillama – an awakening of a person into an ajnir. The term means *awake* in the ancient tongue of Urshan Dai.

arthanti – a gem which gives an ajnir access to the Dinjin for a short period of time

cagma – a monetary coin used on Urshan Dai, a standard unit of money

clinus – an alcoholic drink, popular in Valyna

Drogham – nomadic merchants who dwell in the Kiopic Desert

ekastha – a subtle mental barrier that exists between the three universes. The ajnir breaks through the ekastha to have his experiences with the Dinjin.

Eroma – Mandian name for the lost half of Urshan Dai

Eroni – upper-class Valynans

felmir – a type of stone prevalent on Urshan Dai, commonly used for building

Ganir – the most ancient language of Urshan Dai, spoken by a civilization in the area of current-day Kira Mandi. The language is thought to have mystical properties by the ajnir.

Gargol – Anatami word for *civilization*

gargul – insult of the Mazag residents

Gomex – a red gem

gorlon birds – vulture-like birds that live around Simkada

Gortag – the Great Fault, the location where Urshan Dai split in two

grya – a unit of time on Urshan Dai, about five earthly minutes

Haalathrom – planet in the Dinjin

Dinjin – One of two universes that influences Urshan Dai. It is a world of light and energy, a place where the inhabitants primarily communicate via telepathy.

Janda – a popular spice drink in Simkada

kaliy – a Mandian spice drink

kaaraadruun – a type of mud used on Urshan Dai to build their homes and huts

Kira Mandi – city to remote west of Simkada, an impoverished place on the edge of the Great Fault, where the planet was split

Kurieme – a species of plant on Urshan Dai

Light Star – the sun that lights the world of Urshan Dai

Mazag – the other dimension, besides the Dinjin, which influences the world of Urshan Dai, a world of darkness, terror, pestilence, and famine

Maztacs – a civilization that lives on Haalathrom

Moogies – astral entities that disturb telepathy

namiz – the word for an *omen* in the ajnir language

navkles – nesting birds that live near Simkada
pafnegu – a species of tree on Urshan Dai
Port Authority – the central government of Simkada
Ralisk – wealthy section of Kira Mandi
ralka – game of dice in Simkada
sahala – Mandian word for Dinjin
Sight readers – divination experts in Simkada
Simkada – city of Nadan's birth
sitosis – cloak of a Mandian
subjoia – serum used by the Wheel of Thought to punish its opponents
Tabaci – incense like sandalwood
Tunivial – a perfume worn by Simkadan women
uriel – a type of apparition which speaks in strange, broken riddles
Valyna – city to the north of Simkada, the planet's booming commercial metropolis
Vanil – a type of incense like jasmine
Watching – an intuitive state of mind used by ajnir to find answers to their questions
Zaltin – working class in Valyna

About the Author

 M.P. Gunderson gradu-
ated from Middlebury
College in 1999 with a
degree in Classics. Since
that time, he has worked
as a reporter for a variety
of newspapers in New
England, including *The Community Newspaper Co.*,
The New Hampshire Union Leader, *The New England
Center for Investigative Reporting*, and *The Boston
Globe*. He also writes poetry and studies metaphysics in his spare time. He began work on *The Ajnir* in
2003 under the working title of *The Half Planet*.

*9 7 8 1 6 1 8 5 2 0 3 4 0 *